ASCENSION

FAITH & DEED

BOOK 1

T. KULP

Ascension
© 2026 by T. Kulp

First Edition

ISBN: 978-1-956612-49-3 (ebook)

ISBN: 978-1-956612-53-0 (paperback)

ISBN: 978-1-956612-56-1 (audio)

Published by Making Adventure

16944 York Rd, Suite 62

Monkton, MD 21111

For those on the mountain, and those who have

yet to find their way there.

CONTENT WARNING

Ascension is a work of horror that explores faith, addiction, manipulation, and survival in a dark, modern, realistic fantasy. It contains material that may be distressing to some readers.

Reader discretion is advised.

AUTHOR'S NOTE

In my life today, many know me as a techie and horror writer. The idea that I was someone before this seems unfathomable. That I could have been a completely different person seems to be truly disturbing to people and when the techie/horror writer surface cracks, and the shadows of a former self leak through— people are left to wonder if they know me at all.

My wife, who knows me better than anyone in the world, insists there are at least three Tims. Work sees one Tim. You all see another. And there is at least one Tim buried in time— no longer relevant to the life I've built (nothing dramatic—just a Martial Arts obsessed Tim who doesn't fit in with a life of family, writing, and work). Other Tims float around, surfacing as needed and then again descending below the stormy seas within me. Each Tim has its purpose and they are all me—or I am all of them.

But isn't this everyone?

I can't count how many times I've experienced this myself. We have who we see in a person which is a construct of who we want them to be, who they show us they are, and the tickling deep within our mind that knows who they really are regardless of what we're told or what we're presented.

And to make things even more complicated, there's the challenge of meeting someone in their Chapter 1 or trying to recognize them in their Chapter 50 when the last time you saw them was back in Chapter 10.

This is where Sister Wendy's story begins. In this book she is in—well, for now we'll say, her Chapter 1. And that chapter is not a pleasant one. In *Early Birds Pay Double*, we first encounter Sister Wendy in the flesh as a disturbing, enigmatic, pseudo religious figure who wants to get into Neil's house. Wendy faces Annabelle who rightfully is suspect and even fearful of the woman (and that says something considering the monsters within Annabelle).

Of all the characters I've written, I think Sister Wendy is one of the most interesting. Her world is one of inescapable nightmares, euphoric dreams, mythic powers, and gritty realities.

In the Lazarus Spiral series, I find a few characters create the celestial objects that define gravity and trajectory for the series. Sister Wendy, or as you'll come to know her in this book, Wendy Holowitz, is one of those celestial bodies. She appears heavily in RETURN POLICY (Lazarus Spiral Book 4) and as her gravity sucks in those around her. Is she a black hole leading to annihilation or a gateway to paradise? I'm not sure yet.

ON FAITH & DEED

Originally, the vision for Sister Wendy was to have a single book holding all her stories. But as I wrote, more and more appeared and soon a single book would not work. This original single book was to be called FAITH & DEED.

My Early Readers voted and requested that her tales be splintered into multiple books and that she be given the range, depth, and breadth she deserved.

Thus, here we are. Thank you to my Early Readers who inspired me to go further, think deeper, and unleash the true world of Sister Wendy, the Sylvan Order, The Sleep House, and another major celestial body in the Lazarus Spiral—Mr. Dream.

Why call this series Faith & Deed? Well, it will be obvious as you go along in the stories. Just remember, the Sister Wendy we meet in Early Birds Pay Double and in the Epilogue of Passages is the Chapter 50 Sister Wendy. Here, we are back to Chapter 1…well, sort of. You'll see through the series.

Remember, we are all more than we appear on the page. The Sister Wendy you know from before, is just getting started in this book.

I hope you enjoy.
Tim Kulp
Baltimore, MD
8/26/2025

ASCENSION

ONE

Wendy couldn't lift her head, so she lowered her eyes to meet Death's glare. As she did, the sludge of sweat and vomit smeared over the floorboards mounded up against her lips.

"Come on," she rasped, not sure her lips were moving until the cold, acidic slurry from the floor slipped into her mouth. "Come on." She spat.

Rancid air filmed over her swollen tongue. That stench came from the Basement Dwellers and now, it soaked into her flesh, her ragged clothes, her matted hair.

There was little between the basement door and her roach-infested nest under the stairs except a small foyer. No one dared get too close to the basement. They feared the Basement Dwellers, almost as much as they feared her. Like the basement, no one dared get too close to her.

Death sat only a few feet away, just beyond the open basement door. His pale face split with a wide smile. Drool slid down yellow teeth. Bloody silk sleeves rode high as he delighted in her spasms, her desperate animalistic pleading for him to come.

Her life, the shitty blur she could remember, should be replaying before her eyes. That's what happens. People see their life flash before their eyes right before Death takes them. But the bastard wasn't so kind as to show her the horrid nightmares of her childhood, or the years of addiction, instead Death showed her Cassie.

Cassie – warm once, alive once, and then…Wendy killed her. Wendy tried not to see her final friend, but her mind had teeth sharper than Death's, hungrier, and those teeth gnawed at her bones. Digging in. Grinding down. Forcing her to see the sweet woman rot away.

Cassie could have run.

Cassie could have saved herself.

Cassie could've—

Wendy swallowed the sludge oozing over her lips. It was wet and cold and the only thing she'd been able to swallow in days. Her throat cracked at the relief of anything wet sliding down it. There was no water or food for someone cast under the stairs. Pariah.

Inside her ribs, a parasite coiled, feeding on the sludge. It pulsed within her, searching for gaps in her bones to punch through papery skin – to overtake her.

The parasite, the growth, had been there a long time.

She couldn't remember a time when it wasn't there – after

finding her mother's body, after her mom's boyfriend sold her like the disposal thing she was, after addiction, after years of blissful numbness? Or was it always there? Waiting behind her teeth since she learned how to keep quiet. Sometimes it spoke to her. Whispers reminding Wendy of how thorough the rot was within her. Beyond her body. Deeper than her mind. A rotten soul. Infected. Infectious.

Whether the rot made the growth or the growth made the rot, Wendy didn't care. Wherever it came from, it filled her with more than sadness, more than dope-sick misery. It confirmed that she was so disgusting, so corrupted, even Death wouldn't touch her.

And that is why Death simply sat beyond the basement's open door. Laughing his wet, gurgling laughs. He beckoned her to come. To join him with the Basement Dwellers. To be with those as foul as her.

Something heavy moved on the stairs above her.

Footsteps.

God was coming down from heaven. His blinding white light of judgement preceded him.

Death descended into the dark of the basement.

Wendy tried again to lift her face. God could save her. Just a bit of his Grace could save her. She pressed her leaden arms against the floor, lifting her face from the sludge with a wet sucking. Her lashes stuck together where they were immersed.

"Rise my faithful!" God called. "I bring you Grace and the word of your Lord. Rise! Rise and give me an amen!"

Shambling bodies slithered to the foyer. The ruined and the fresh alike lay prostrate before him. "Amen," the others moaned, a chorus of need. Hands lifted. Faces pressed into the fuzzy mold covered foyer.

Wendy's brain screamed, *God commands you to come, speak, do something!* But her body did nothing.

Too weak to obey your God. Weak of body. Weak of faith. So pathetic, the growth said.

God's halo devoured the shadows, driving the Basement Dwellers—even Death himself back into their pit.

His white suit wasn't worn but conjured—woven from light itself. A crimson tie spilled down his chest, vanishing into his gleaming vest. Even his shoes glowed white.

As always, a man followed behind God. He held a spotlight to illuminate God for all to bask in his blinding judgement.

"Deliverance has come!" God called. He scoffed, commanding his light to move further behind him. Satisfied, he continued, "Before the good news of your Lord, may I give you Grace?"

No one answered. They simply raised their quivering hands higher.

God's light didn't reach Wendy's ashy flesh. The growth in her, the pulsing sore, reminded her again and again of her weakness. She strained to prove it wrong, to make her body do something. Faith demanded she respond to God.

Her body was weak. Her faith was not.

Her faith in the power of others had never been weak.

God could heal her. His Grace would heal her.

Wendy's elbow trembled. Her arm flopped out, clanging against metal.

Her Bionic Woman lunchbox.

Once it held the Grace she saved—now only wriggling roaches. They crawled over her as nothing more than one of them.

God threw baggies of Grace to the faithful. Fingers snatched. Teeth tore plastic. Graying tongues swiped powder. The frenzy filled the foyer—wet smacks, stuttered breaths, the little sob that could have been delight or despair.

God smiled and said, "Yes. Take, eat of me."

He dropped a bag at his feet. A woman grabbed it. He stamped down on her hand, smiling, grinding his foot through her cracking bones. "Life does not consist of abundance. Have the Grace in your hand before taking another."

God kicked her away.

The baggie in her ruined hand skittered and spun across the floorboards, stopping near Wendy's hand.

God's light made his Grace glow, pale as moonlight.

She could reach it.

Wendy's fingers crept across the floor. Her cragged nails digging through splinters to pull herself to salvation. The pain should've registered. It didn't. All she had was the distance between her and the Grace, her life and Death.

A young woman darted for the baggie. She froze when her eyes met Wendy's.

The young woman had none—she was fresh, hooked on the Grace; not yet ruined by it. The woman whimpered.

Fear shook the woman harder than her need. No one crossed *The Beast Under the Stairs*. That's what the others called Wendy in hushed voices they thought she never heard. The name fit. It kept everyone away from her.

It kept this woman away from Wendy's Grace. The thing she needed to stay alive just one more day. But the woman was soft and fresh – how Cassie began. The Sleep House hadn't ruined her yet. She could still leave – she could run. Maybe this hit would be what gave her the strength to go. To save herself.

Like Cassie should have.

Wendy turned her eyes away. The woman snatched the Grace and shrank back.

"Now, for our news. Three of you have been chosen to ascend beyond the Sleep House! Those pure of faith shall go forth into the world and share my Gospel."

This was how God spoke of Ascension. Ascending beyond the darkness of the Sleep House to the world beyond.

Last Ascension, three people left.

None came back.

The time before that, three left.

None returned.

God's gaze swept over them, bored. "Ascension is an honor for those who truly believe."

In the Sleep House, most people wanted Grace. Wendy wanted *absolution*. She believed in God, and that faith burned in her chest. It writhed in her chest, coiling and uncoiling, fueling her muscles, giving her fingers the strength to drag her from under the stairs into God's light.

God selected a man and a woman. Quick. Careless.

Then his eyes caught Wendy. Her ghastly form slithered from her nest.

"You!" he said.

She froze.

God saw her. Chose her.

His faith in her, that she was worthy of Ascension, turned

her arms to steel, dragged breath back into her lungs. She lifted her face to his, pleading wordlessly for Grace.

Just a taste.

Just enough to make her tongue work, to say, *Throw me out. Please. Don't feed me to the Basement Dwellers,* which God did to those who died in the Sleep House.

God knelt, smiling peacefully at her.

"Are you at the end my child?" he asked.

Wendy's body tried to weep at the words *my child,* but there were no tears left in her – just dry grit behind her eyes.

He dangled a baggie just above her fingertips, making her reach. Making her show him, show everyone, her desperation.

"Do you remember the sins that led you here? I do."

He motioned to the staircase then to the basement door. Disgust twisted his face.

A memory swept over him, releasing his disgust. God sat with the memory. Wendy had only blurred memories of the Sleep House. All hazed with pure numbness brought by Grace. She wondered what moved behind his eyes, deep in his mind, in his light.

He breathed out, satisfied. "But redemption is nigh, and you, child shall leave the Sleep House to spread my grandeur."

He dropped the bag in her palm, forcing her to shut around

it. Then he shoved her with his foot – hard – under the stairs. She slid over the filth, popping roaches as she smacked the wall behind her.

As God started up the stairs, he spoke over his shoulder.

"Clean them up. I don't want the buyer to question their durability."

Buyer?

The word slid through her like the slurry on the floor. But questions were the root of her sin, so she left them.

Ascension. Proof of her faith.

A way out from under the stairs, back to the Sleep House Library. A way back to God's Grace. Perhaps, Wendy dared, a way to make Cassie's name stop tasting like rot in her mouth.

Penance. Salvation.

But failing Ascension…her eyes glanced to the basement doorway. Death was gone – for now. He'd return if she failed. And Cassie's death would have been for nothing.

On the first floor, among the mortals, Wendy curled around her Grace. She smeared a pinky full on her gums.

The powder hit her blood and sang.

Warmth flooded her few remaining teeth. Her belly unclenched. The world softened at the edges, just enough for a long exhale to flow from her.

Darkness settled over her eyes like wet wool.

Sleep took her in a way Death refused: quickly.

TWO

Two men came for Wendy. God sent them to prepare her for Ascension, so she didn't fight.

"Easy," one of them said, as if she were a ravenous dog.

He groped for her in the darkness under the stairs. She presented her arm to ease his work and permit him purchase without him seeking his own. His fingers closed around her arm and pulled her from under the stairs.

She slid out on the sludge, ripped from beneath the stairs, slick and encrusted as a newborn.

"Eww!" The grabber said and dropped her arm as she slid towards him. "Fuckin' gross."

"Shit, I thought this one was half-wolf from how the others talk about her," the other man, unbothered by the filth, hooked around her waist and threw Wendy over his shoulder.

"Ya'gonna listen to junk heads? What the fuck they know?" The man carrying her said. He wore heavy black boots.

As they walked out, he kicked a woman in the foyer. She made a small sound—more air than voice—and curled tighter around her baggie of Grace. Boot man cawed laughter.

Outside, the cool numbness of the Sleep House gave way to heavy, oppressive heat.

The thick humidity didn't taste like the Sleep House. No sour breath. No spoiled food. No human rot soaked into moldy wood. This air—briny wind off water and diesel made her tongue curl in then stretched to taste more.

A city sat beyond the warehouses that surrounded the Sleep House. Lights twinkled. Distant. Unreachable. Wendy couldn't remember which city it was. Couldn't remember arriving? Only water somewhere close, and boat horns moaning through the night like tortured spirits.

She'd always thought those moans came from the Basement Dwellers – but now seeing the lights, hearing the water, she remembered the boats.

Her throat tightened at the missing memory. When did she come here? How?

The men took her between the Sleep House, little more than a blighted row house, and a collapsing shed. The ground sucked at their boots.

Then they dropped her.

Freezing muddy slop swallowed her face. She turned her head to breathe. Mud slid into her mouth. The wet, gritty grime was the first thing she had down her throat in days that wasn't vomit. She slurped again to get the water, the little bit of water, into her body.

Boot man, the one who had carried her—the one who kicked the woman, ripped her ragged clothes away. Fabric tore. Humid air weighed down across her naked back.

Wendy's eyes found his.

Nothing else moved.

"Shit," Boot man yelped.

He staggered away.

Wendy didn't smile—not with her mouth. She couldn't. But her eyes sharpened, pleading him to come closer. To touch her again. Try it.

His gaze stayed where it should—on her eyes, on her threat—rather than sliding over her body. Fear held his leash. Nothing kept ideas from the minds of men like fear.

"Did you see that?" he whispered.

His partner fussed with a garden hose. "See what?" He didn't look at Wendy. He didn't look at anything he might have to admit was a person.

"I—nothing I guess," Boot man said, his voice went small.

Hose man cranked the faucet. The metal squealed.

Then the spray hit Wendy with sharp teeth scouring away the filth, driving out her breath. Grime ran from her in gray streams. Mud broke apart in clots, surging around her face.

She tried to gasp.

The spray rushed into her mouth. Into her nose.

She choked—throat spasming. The pressure wouldn't let the water soak into her, only rush over her, through her. A scream swelled, then broke apart beneath the jet of water, washed away with the grime. As she choked on her cries, her eyes stabbed through the gray filth streaming from her to watch her tormentors. She'd die before giving a moment of power to these men.

"Roll her over," Hose man shouted.

Boot man didn't move.

Wendy lay still; eyes locked onto Boot man. as the stream was redirected to the puddle beside her face.

"Let's get this shit over with man," Hose man said. "I got other shit to do."

Boot man edged closer, approaching her like roadkill-unsure if it was dead or waiting to bite.

"I'm just gonna roll you over, okay?" he said.

Wendy's stare did the talking her throat couldn't.

Boot man shivered – receiving the message.

He gently turned her shoulders, then rolled her to her back. Mud clung to her in cold blotches, but she didn't shiver. Grace still warmed her blood—dull, stubborn warmth under all this cold.

Her breasts pointed into the night. She didn't try to cover herself. Shame didn't buy anything here – it never did.

"Damn," hose man said. "Kinda hot for a strung-out bitch,"

Boot man blushed and looked away.

Hose man barked, "Stand her up."

Boot man obeyed, hands trembling. Not from her physical weight—she weighed nothing—but from the sense of something else, something packed into her skin, deep in her bones. He held her under the arms. Wendy towered over him by a few inches.

"I'm sorry," Boot man said, barely a whisper under the water.

Wendy didn't answer.

Hose man sprayed her down. Muddy crust dribbled off her at first in waves, then in drips as the hose squeaked off.

The silence was as suffocating as the humidity.

"Take her to the shed," Hose man commanded.

Boot man lifted Wendy carefully, like a child. His eyes flicked to hers, then to the baggie still trapped in her fist.

Wendy followed his glance. Grace. The only thing that made her muscles remember what they were for. She clenched it tighter, ready to kill him if he got any ideas.

But he didn't.

As she knew it would, fear kept all ideas out of his head.

He set her inside the shed and said, "I'm going to put you in here, okay?"

He did so carefully. Then stepped away slowly, watching her eyes for any hint of her intentions. None could be gleaned.

"Why you askin'?" Hose man scoffed from the doorway. "Just dump the bitch."

Boot man's attention stayed on Wendy's stare.

She knew that look. Not empathy. Not care.

It asked, *"are we okay?"* Not if *she* was okay. Never that.

Boot man needed to know the predator wouldn't turn on him. Needed to believe kindness bought safety. Wendy could taste his fear – sharp, clean, alive.

It tasted like power. Like a cookie, sweet and delicious.

Hose man lowered his voice, "Did you hear what's going on? We gettin' a cut this time? Is this like—"

Boot man cut him off, "No, not like that." His words came quick, urgent. "They would have gotten fresher meat. This is… some kind of hunting thing. I don't know. Rich people do weird shit." He swallowed. "Keep your mouth shut. Maybe we'll get a tip or something."

Inside the shed, the other candidates for Ascension, the man and woman, rocked in separate corners. Each held themselves together by clenching Grace in their fists.

Wendy scurried into an empty corner and began doing the same.

Boot man came back with a white jumpsuit. Clean. Bright. Like God's suit, but cheap and thin. He dressed Wendy in it with fast hands, eyes everywhere but her skin. The other two already wore theirs, zipped to the throat.

"What the hell man?" Hose man said. "You want to kiss her before we go? She'd be hot if she ate a fuckin' sandwich – got the roaches out her hair."

He laughed, never looking in her eyes.

Boot man didn't laugh. He finished zipping Wendy's suit and escaped the shed.

Outside he took a deep breath and rolled his shoulders — putting his tough-guy mask back on as if he were now the alpha predator.

Hose man shut the shed door.

The lock clicked.

Wendy woke to shouting.

"I'll kill you!" the man screamed.

The woman shrank away, curled into a tight ball. A high-pitched whimper came from her.

Wendy knew that whimper.

She'd heard it. She'd made it. More times than she could count.

Her shivers stopped.

Something inside her stirred, the pulsing growth, the thing that made her The Beast Under the Stairs.

Tangy adrenaline laced the spit filling her mouth. She swallowed, smiling without showing any teeth.

She slid closer to him, quiet as a knife slicing flesh.

Wendy whispered, "What will God do to a sinner like you?" Her voice rasped. Her throat relearning how to talk. "For killing his chosen. What will he do? Strike you down."

A small giggle, dripping with malicious glee, escaped her.

The man's eyes snapped to Wendy. He knew of her. What that giggle meant, the horrors it held for him.

But he was chosen too. Wendy had already infuriated God enough; she dared not hurt his chosen. She stopped, too far to reach him, to kill him, and merely hissed at him.

"Smite!" the other woman whispered, shaking.

"Smite!" Wendy echoed, throwing the word like a stone.

He flinched. Cowered.

God had rained smite before. Wendy had seen him stomp a man to death, then have the man's lover lick the gore from his white shoes until they glowed. Then commanded the lover to take the body to the basement. Neither was seen nor heard from again.

Cruelty and Grace. Given from the same hand. Given with the same smile.

Wendy had sinned. She'd earned Smite. But God had only cast her from the Library to under the stairs, not into the basement, not to Death.

The man yelped and shrank away.

The woman scooted closer, mistaking danger for protection.

Cassie was Wendy's last friend. There would be no other.

Wendy shook her head.

The woman stopped. Shifted away.

Minutes dragged. The shed creaked and settled around them. Eventually the man's fear burned into exhaustion. He slumped. The woman's shaking slowed.

They drifted back to sleep,

Wendy followed.

A dream came.

The Sleep House didn't allow dreams when Grace held you. Grace made you blank and floating. Here, in the shed, they were beyond God's protection. Wendy's mind slipped its leash.

In the dream she was strong.

A warrior. A queen.

God lay dead at her feet. His light snuffed out. Justice served by her hand. She smiled.

Around Wendy knelt an army of sweat-slick black flesh and horned heads, smoke wreathing their thick muscles. They bowed as the faithful did to God, but when they looked up, they wore glossy white masks with no faces.

The horizon burned ember-orange.

A wave of monks in green cloaks charged across it, screaming prayers.

Wendy lifted her hand.

She slashed it down.

The monks screamed, crushed under the invisible forces she wielded. The screams changed from human to animal, to gurgling in their own pulpy gore.

Wendy cackled laughter.

Joy coiled, pulsing in her breast—hot, bright, ancient. She couldn't remember joy like this – power like this, yet it felt so familiar. Magic. She knew it in the dream without knowing how.

She walked through monks. Her steps squished and squelched over the congealing mounds of gore that were once people. Black smoke billowed from her, blanketing the world in shadows deeper than the Sleep House basement.

She kicked over the flapping flesh remains of a monk, laughing until she saw the boneless face, the smear of flesh and brains, was her face.

She froze.

She looked around.

Every monk—every fallen body—was her ruined face.

The masked army rose.

Hands reached up.

Then the masks were peeled away.

Under them: her. Her. Her. Hungry copies smiling with her mouth. Her lips parting, peeling away from curling needle teeth.

They closed in.

Wendy tried to run.

The dead grabbed her ankles. Flabby flesh tendrils coiling over her feet, slithering up her legs. Too many. Cold. Insistent. Pulling her down as if the earth itself was swallowing her.

They bit.

They fed.

Wendy screamed straight into a creature's gaping maw, her cry drowned in the drool spilling down her throat.

A young woman's hand broke through the darkness in a ray of light—reaching for Wendy, fingers stretching desperate to hook onto her.

Wendy reached.

Their fingertips touched. The woman's hand curled into hers.

Then a monk in black stepped into the light and—clean as a thought, sharp as doubt—cut the woman's hand off.

The hand fell away.

The light went with it.

The woman vanished into shadow. Had she never existed?

Wendy knew her. Called for her.

But the woman was gone.

The dead devoured her.

The man with the sword stood over her, hefting his curved blade high over her heart. She spit at him, still fighting the dead as their mouths tore her away.

He laughed, wet, joyless, filling the world. He plunged the sword down. It thudded through her heart in a bright flash of heat, of light, dissolving the world in white nothing.

Wendy woke with a silent gasp, hand clamped over her chest where the sword should have been.

She jumped to her feet, her blood pumping, the muscles in her body finally fueled after years of atrophy.

Where was the sword?

Where was the man in black? The faithful?

The masks?

Gone.

The shed door groaned opened.

Wendy snapped toward it, to face the man in black.

He was coming for her.

He was here—*again*?

Again…again, meant history. Again, meant she'd seen him before – and didn't she know him? Hadn't she recognized him and the woman in the dream?

Hadn't she?

Questions scattered as God's light spilled into the shed, white and absolute.

Wendy's knees hit the floor.

She lay at his feet.

The dream of God's death, her joy in killing him, collapsed under the reality of Ascension—and the thin hope, stupid and bright, that she might earn her way back into Grace.

THREE

"Rise my children," God said.

Wendy's legs answered before her mind finished hearing him. She pushed up fast, ankles screaming tight as wire, head spinning from rising too quickly. But she swallowed the pain, the faintness, to show God her strength.

The other woman tried to stand. Failed. Her knees collapsed under her. Wendy caught her under the arm and hauled her upright. The woman's bones felt hollow in Wendy's grip.

"For God's sake," Wendy croaked. "Stand. Do what he said."

The man was worse. He wobbled on his knees, shaking, lips quivering around nothing. Wendy lurched to him, yanked him to his feet. He sagged against her like soaked rags.

These two won't make it.

They couldn't even stand when commanded. How could they Ascend anything?

God spoke quickly and nervously, his eyes jutting about the shed. "I will exit and bring with me the vessel of your Ascension. Be focused. Be aware. Present yourselves well my children."

Without looking at them, he left.

They stood in a line, Wendy at one end, the woman at the other. Together they held up the man. Each held their hands behind them, clenching their last bits of Grace.

Outside, two men argued. Their voices were muffled through the plywood walls. A deep voice barked, and the talking stopped.

Silence.

The door opened.

God entered. No light. Just a white suit, radiant as a dying star.

Another man followed him in. A brown cloak draped over his massive body as if a mountain floated behind God. The hood was up, casting a stern face in deep shadow. Only the hard line of a beard showed—dark and neatly cut.

Wendy's stomach dropped.

Her dream flashed behind her eyes. The curved blade. The man in black's wet gurgling laughter, the word *again* catching in her throat.

This wasn't a dream.

He'd throw her to the ground, draw his sword, and run her through. The others would sink their teeth into her throat.

She'd try to scream but would only gargle, drowning in the metallic sludge of her own gnawed flesh and blood.

She could fight – but he was a mountain, and if this was the will of God, so be it. If she fought, she would be denied Ascension. She'd be cast into the basement, or worse, left alive and sent away from the Sleep House and then what?

Nowhere else to go, a growl rolled up from the growth under her ribs, familiar and hungry. *Nowhere you belong.*

Wendy locked her knees. Held herself tall. She forced the nothing in her stomach to stay down. She wouldn't retch in front of God.

The monk lowered his hood.

No mask. No sword. Just a finely trimmed brown beard, short wavy hair, and eyes severe, disciplined, punishing.

Wendy knew many men with those eyes. They punished first and asked questions later. Men who liked the sound of *yes*.

Her eyes, determined, hard, met his.

"I am Acolyte Horn," he said, his voice calm in a way that made Wendy's skin prickle. Too peaceful to have eyes like those. "I'm told you are the best of his family."

He stepped close enough for Wendy to smell him through the clots of mud in her nose. Soap. Leather. Something clean—fresh, pine.

"Open your mouth," Horn said.

Wendy's eyes flicked to God.

He nodded…but he hesitated, uncertain?

How could God be uncertain of anything?

He wanted this to be over. Fast. To return to the Sleep House.

Wendy opened her mouth.

Horn glanced in and went to the man beside her then repeated his command. Then the woman.

When he returned to Wendy he stared at her face, not in her eyes, but seeing all of her without moving his head.

"When did you come here?" Horn asked.

Wendy tried to cast her mind through the haze of time but only found broken images: her mother's arm dangling out from motel tub, water and flesh gone gray; the clacking of her bike chain as she raced home from one of her mom's 'deliveries'; a hand on the back of her neck, squeezing and sweaty; a man's voice saying *be good* without adding *or else*.

No dates. No numbers. Time didn't exist. The Sleep House peeled it from her.

"I'm not sure, sir," Wendy said.

God nodded approval at her manners.

Horn moved down the line with the same question, each giving an approximate answer matching Wendy's. No one knew when they came, only that they were here.

Horn asked the woman at the end of the line one last question, "Are you ready to be free?" She nodded without looking at God.

The man did the same, eyes glassy.

When asked, Wendy said, "I am free."

Horn's mouth twitched. "Is that so?"

Wendy leveled her chin to him. "I am here for God's Grace," she said. Each word forged carefully in her dry mouth to avoid coughing, choking, scratching. Clarity would present her well. "I will fulfill his commandments until I can no longer do so. I am not a prisoner. I'm not a slave. I'm a follower."

Horn laughed – loud, surprised, like she'd just shared a joke he didn't expect.

Wendy didn't flinch. She presented herself well, still, polite. Once, laughter like that would've let the thing pulsing under her ribs out. It would have wreaked havoc. Feasting on blood and fear and panic.

Fragments of memory warmed her insides—of holding a gore-drenched broken pen, standing in a motel room over a kneeling, middle-aged man. He begged for his life after trying to take hers. Wendy let him scream as she dug out his throat with the plastic pen shards.

But this laughter wasn't mockery. It was amusement.

Horn's laughter faded into a smile. He stepped back, looked Wendy over then said, "This one."

She stood taller to present herself more clearly. Her back popped, hollow and echoing through the shed. All winced, except Horn.

He pointed at her and said, "Where did she come from?"

God shifted. "She came here of her own accord."

Horn waited, eyes on God, for the real answer.

None came.

Silence stretched, thin and uncomfortable.

God said, "And the others?" His voice rose, too bright, losing the certainty Wendy always knew from him. "Would you consider them?"

Horn's gaze cut to the man and woman. He shook his head once. "They will not survive. They can barely stand much less climb."

The words landed heavy, the man buckling but Wendy held him firm. The woman whimpered as she had earlier, but Wendy didn't feel for her this time. Pity didn't keep you alive here – and it wouldn't in Ascension.

Horn didn't look at them again.

He reached into an inner pocket and pulled out a black hood—cloth thick and rough, folded like a tool. He held it out to Wendy.

"I need you to wear this."

Wendy took it. The cloth was coarse burlap. She pulled it over her head.

"God's will be done," she said.

Darkness swallowed her.

Horn said, "Do you want to say goodbye?"

Wendy shook her head once. "I'll return."

She believed it as she said it. Belief was the only thing she had in her that wasn't mud or hunger or rot.

Horn didn't answer.

He guided her toward the door with a hand at her elbow—light, controlled.

The sack's fabric scraped her cheeks. Every inhale dragged in the heavy, oaty stink trapped in the cloth. Not a mask. Not a bag. Something meant to be cinched over an animal's head so it couldn't see where it was going.

Wendy didn't linger on the parallel to her situation. She let it float away before it could bite.

Outside, boots squished in the mud. Two men passed close—Hose man's sharp steps, Boot man's heavier shuffle.

Someone exhaled, long and relieved, as Wendy went by.

Wendy smiled inside the hood.

Behind her, God's voice filled the shed again, confidence snapping back into place like a collar. "Your Ascension begins at the hands of my angels."

A yelp—high and sudden—from the woman.

A wet, choking sound from the man.

Then the shed door closed, and the sounds cut off.

Moonlight leaked through the weave in pale threads. A dark vehicle idled loudly ahead of her. Wendy was steered toward it.

Hands helped her up. Metal under her palms. The floor vibrated with the engine's grumbling. The door slid shut with a final, sealed sound.

In the hood's dark, Wendy held on to one thought the way she held on to her baggie of Grace.

I'll return.

No one ever did.

But then again, no one was ever her.

FOUR

The van ride started smoothly with only the thump of potholes, the rattle of rumble strips. Then the pavement ended, turning the world into gnashing teeth. The tires chewed on rock. The van jostled and bucked.

The hood still reeked of feed—oats and old grains—but another smell pushed through it. Sweet but earthy. One of those pine tree air fresheners her mom kept in their car, before the repo man took it. Wendy tried to ignore the chemical flavor, wishing for more of the oat smell.

The ride itself was almost…nice.

No being stuffed in the trunk. No hands clenching her hair. No voice screaming for her to shut up.

Not that she said anything.

People talked quietly in muffled whispers. A few laughs. One man, young from his tone, asked someone whether they went to a basketball game the other night. The other guy hadn't.

Wendy kept her hands still in her lap, fingers curled around her baggie. Within the hood, her eyes jumped to every voice.

One, two, three, four, she counted each voice and laugh. Two flanked her. One sat across. Another further away.

They all laughed, blurring the count.

This must be part of the test. Comfort as bait.

She stayed sharp, alert, focused.

A wave of dizziness washed over her as if the floor tilted. Her mind slid inside her skull, loose, twisting. The van grew quiet, tense—grunts, shifting weight, someone catching themselves with a hard thump on the van wall. Wendy's stomach lifted.

SLAM! The van hit a hard bump.

Wendy's skull snapped back, cracking against the van wall. White stars popped in the darkness of her hood.

"Sorry," basketball guy said. His hand hovered over her leg, not touching but she could sense it too close. "Are you okay?"

Wendy nodded once.

The hand moved away.

The shakes crawled out of her nerves. Not a tremble. A skittering. Bugs scrambling to tear through her skin. The same bugs that drove Cassie to her death.

Wendy flinched. Cassie's nails raking her own arms raw, scraping and scraping, until the raised welts split into gashes. Blood poured from them, but nothing ever crawled out.

Wendy's breath hitched. Her stomach turned, empty and vicious.

God's Grace was in her fist. It would feed the bugs in her, get them to sleep.

She worked the baggie's seal open with her thumb, dipped a finger—

A hand slapped it out of her grip.

The baggie hit the floor with a soft puff. Powder floated up, too faint to taste. Someone coughed. Someone gagged. A window was opened blasting freezing wind through the van.

"You're done with that life," Horn said.

Horn's voice came from directly across the van. Calm. Commanding. Just as he did at the shed, giving orders to God and expecting God to obey.

Rage coursed through her body. Every muscle tightened, ready to pounce, to claw his eyes out. She'd rip the hood away. Bite. Strangle. The other men were young—boys with confidence and soft bodies, thinking they were men.

They'd be lambs to her slaughter.

Her hands flexed in her lap.

But God gave her to Horn, to these men. Who was she to question God…*again*?

This was all part of God's plan.

She stayed seated.

The jitters surfaced, shaking her harder. Her legs wanted

to jump. Her arms wanted to twist, to jerk, to do anything that might shake the crawling out of her. Her chest was too tight for her ribs.

God had faith in her. He chose her for Ascension.

She held still.

The ride grew rougher.

Then colder.

Freezing air swept through her suit, blowing away all warmth within. A bite crept down her arms. Into her bones. It wasn't the hood making it hard to breathe. The air was thin. Never enough to fill her lungs.

The van slowed.

Stopped.

The door roared open.

Gentle hands lifted Wendy from the van. Soft ground squished under her shoes. The freshness beyond her hood choked her with the smell of crisp air and sap-bleeding trees, wet earth that wasn't soaked in human rot.

"Go to the light," Horn said.

The door slammed.

Tires ground in dirt. The van pulled away, the sound fading.

Wendy tore off the hood.

Trees spotted the slope, tall trunks, not dense, but close

enough to stitch a canopy that hid the stars. The moon peeked around thin clouds, curiously watching Wendy. A storm was brewing in the clean air and dark night. The air tasted like the rumor of rain…a flavor, a memory emerging from the haze of her childhood.

Fog rolled down the mountain in a heavy gray swell, tumbling in the faint moonlight. The sky spilling down the mountain.

The van vanished into it.

Wendy stood there in her white jumpsuit, glowing.

Not bright—no spotlight—but the fabric caught the little moonlight and threw it into the fog. A dull halo clung to her in the mist. Enough to keep her from tripping over the rocks jutting out of the grass.

Enough to make her visible.

A shiver ran through her hard enough to chatter her few teeth.

The sickness came fast now. Cold flashed into heat. Heat into cold, a sheet of ice sliding down her spine. Gooseflesh pulsed over her body, under the suit. Her stomach clenched, folding in on itself.

She didn't see the eyes at first.

She was too busy trying not to fall apart.

"Now what?" she asked the mountain.

No answer.

The swelling fog swallowed her voice, silencing her with the rest of the mountain.

Ascension must involve climbing. That much was simple. Climb. Prove. Endure.

Would that absolve her sins?

Perhaps.

Her legs were frail. Each step slid, the mountain not giving her anything solid to stand upon. The steep slope pulled at her breath with every lurching step. Her glowing suit swung like a puffy lantern, lighting rocks, roots, and patches of slick grass.

She didn't question why her suit was so bright. Questions were the root of her sin. It was light. Light meant guidance— judgment. Light was a gift from God.

Wendy leaned against a tree to catch her breath. The world spun. The shakes had her—deep, full-body tremors rattled her joints. Her feet scuffed in the grass.

A twig snapped. It echoed around her.

She didn't feel it under her foot, but that could have been because her focus on fighting the need to puke.

Nothing rushed out of the fog. No hands. No voices.

Only her own breathing—too loud, too desperate. Each gasp swallowed by the fog, silencing her.

Always check your blind spots, a man's voice echoed—creamy tuna sandwiches and a blooming warm smile flashed in Wendy's mind.

Who—

Her stomach lurched, chasing away the voice, the memory of sandwiches. She swallowed sour spit and tried not to gag.

When was the last time she ate?

She couldn't find it. Not the day. Not the meal. Nothing.

How long had she climbed?

Hours?

Minutes?

Her muscles screamed, but that had little to do with the climb and much to do with the waves of dope sickness crashing over her.

Each step built the sickness as if drawing every hangover, every morning after into her now. Those feelings sagged within her, dragged around her, as if pulling anchors up the mountain.

And yet the strangest sensation tingled around her. The ropes binding those anchors were being sawed away. Relief, freedom, or just death from exhaustion was ahead.

Her lips cracked. Bled. Dehydrated as she saw the first pulsing blue light.

It wasn't far.

Had it been there the whole time?

Go to the light, Horn said.

So, she did.

Blue lights like that flashed in parking lots. Emergency phones. Police-call boxes. Not that Wendy would ever touch one. Blue lights were for people who wanted to be found. People who had answers ready. People who didn't flinch when someone asked their name.

People who were used to the dark, people like her, didn't go towards the blue lights.

But it was the only light. And so, she climbed.

She hugged herself, rubbing her arms to feel something more than numbness. Her body wouldn't run – not like this, not after years of rot and hunger and Grace. So, she stumbled forward with stiff legs, tight lungs, and a clenched gut.

The blue light led her into a small clearing.

A campsite was waiting, set up for her.

A tray. A bottle of thick white liquid. A glass of water. Two pills. Notes on scraps of paper, words written in blunt marker like commands.

Drink this.

Drink this too.

Swallow with the white drink.

One more note lay under everything, pinned by the tray's weight.

You'll need all of this. Ascension lies ahead. Drink. Swallow. Rest.

Wendy stared at the bottle.

The liquid inside was chalky and thick, clinging to the plastic when she tipped it. The water smelled like nothing—clean, blank.

Her hands shook as she picked up the pills, tossing them down her throat. She lifted the white drink, pausing.

A trick. Poison. Something meant to make her easier. Weaker.

Her belly cramped. The shakes surged.

Defiance was useless if she couldn't move. Maybe the pills were Grace?

She chased them down her throat with the white drink.

Warm. Smooth.

Vanilla.

The taste hit the back of her throat and yanked a memory up so fast a bolt of pain lanced her mind.

Her mom. An ice cream shop. Bright lights and buzzing signs. A counter that smelled sweet. Mom laughing—real, not broken. Hair pinned up. Clothes clean. Wendy holding a little spoon. Sample after sample. Her mom nudging her to say *not this* one like it was their secret game.

For a moment, Wendy could see it so clearly, she forgot the fog and the mountain.

Then the memory slid away, and her throat tightened to cry, but nothing came.

She washed out the sweetness in her mouth with the water until her spit was sour, tasting like herself again.

Down the mountain, a shout cracked through the mist, then laughter.

Wendy's spine went rigid, perking up to hear clearly.

They laughed again.

She turned her head slightly, listening hard, pushing her attention down the slope the way she used to push her attention down alleys. Fog swallowed everything. Smells died in the damp cold. Her ears had to do the work as they did in the van.

Three, maybe four voices. Talking sports. Teasing. Loud enough to carry.

The men from the van.

Horn, if he was down there, didn't say anything.

Branches rustled close by.

Wendy snapped her gaze toward the sound.

The rustling stopped.

Slowly, deliberately, the pressure of eyes watching her crawled over her skin. The air changed as it did when being gawked at, being wanted, being prey. Wendy knew the feelings. She'd lived them so long.

The clearing was open. Trees ringing it, but not close enough to hide someone. The mountain fell away to steep emptiness beyond the campsite.

The fog could hide her.

Not with this suit glowing.

Another burst of laughter tugged her attention downslope. The blue light pulsed in the corner of her vision—steady as a heartbeat. A calm heartbeat.

It was a beacon.

A beacon for her.

Or for them.

Wendy found the switch and clicked it off.

Darkness rushed in, immediate and thick. Under the stairs she knew this darkness but here it stretched forever. Only the moon cast a faint silver sheen over the world but even that faded behind a cloud.

The world had vanished. Darkness bloomed around her—like her dream. The faithful in her dream billowing up around her, engulfing her.

In the dark, she saw the truth.

Hunting.

That's what Boot man and Hose man were talking about. Sport. Rich people. Tips.

This was Ascension.

They weren't driving her up here to save her.

They were turning her loose.

Wendy's chest tightened. She collapsed in the wet grass, holding her breath until her shaking eased, until the clouds broke and the moon was returned to the world.

Wendy whispered, "You cannot stop me."

She rolled to her stomach and stared up the mountain.

Her hunger softened with the white drink, her throat soothed by the water, she began climbing again.

No rest.

Only Ascension.

She moved quietly, keeping her head angled downslope to catch the shape of their laughter through the fog.

She didn't notice the eyes.

Didn't hear the soft, wet press of something stepping where grass should have been silent.

The men weren't the only ones following.

Something else kept to the trees, matching her climb without a word. Saliva trickled around their mouths as they watched tonight's feast stumble up the mountain.

FIVE

When was the last time Wendy had eaten?

Her mind reached for an answer. None was found. Only the taste of bile and old powdery Grace.

The thick white drink sat heavy in her. Full. Warm. Wrong. In the Sleep House, full didn't exist. Meals didn't exist. Nor mealtime. Not even the concept of time. Sometimes someone dropped a pile of feed from the dumpsters in the foyer. You ate what you could before the hands and teeth closed in. But even then, food was something you did fast to get it over with. It was only a distraction from the numbness of God's Grace.

And water—real water. When did she last have clean water? Not a coke, not the gray grimy bowls put out for them, but clean, cold water.

The mountain's moisture soaked into her. Mist clung to her suit, her skin, loosening her crusty matted black hair. Color crept back into her ashen hands. Muscles that had been brittle and creaking began to stretch, lubricated by hydration.

She was sore – bone to skin, but the ache felt good. It meant she was using herself again.

Awake.

Alive.

The next blue light waited ahead.

A larger bottle of water sat beside it. Nothing else. No tray. No notes. No pills. Wendy crouched and searched the ground anyway, dragging her gaze over the wet grass and rocks.

No footprints.

She left prints in the mud around the beacon, yet whoever brought the water had left none. No crushed grass. No scuffed streaks. Like they hadn't walked here at all.

Or had erased their tracks?

She sipped the water.

Beyond the canopy above, clouds broke releasing a flood of moonlight.

She glowed in the fog.

Her jumpsuit was like a flashlight.

No—worse.

Her stomach sank, the truth shoving it down. The pulsing growth under her ribs coiling and unwrapping…laughing within her. The suit wasn't for her to see.

It was for her to *be seen*.

For the hunters.

Wendy swallowed hard. "I don't make anything easy," she repeated what her mom always said about her. But unlike her mom, Wendy wasn't frazzled, wasn't cracking.

She knelt. Scooped a handful of mud and smeared it across her suit. The glow dulled. She layered it, clump after clump, until her suit was more mud than cloth.

She clicked off the blue light.

The mud and dark dimmed her—less a star, more a pale cloud drifting through the haze.

A branch snapped nearby.

Wendy froze.

The sharp crack—the sudden hush that followed—lit every nerve in her.

Fog coiled around her. Inhuman grins formed as the gray mists swirled and rose. The mountain was hiding something from her. Those grins were it laughing at the hidden, horrible secret she'd discover all too late.

Down the slope a real laugh broke through the mists. The laughter of men. Closer. Heavier. The lightness and fun fading as their hunt closed in.

An animal growled.

Silenced by the mountain. The laughing still echoed. The mountain wanted her to hear that, but not the growl. Not the…

Bears?

Bears were the worst thing a mountain could hold, right? People and bears. In that order. That was the whole list of dangers here. Other animals might be around – but nothing worse than bears. Nothing worse than men.

She couldn't imagine worse, yet.

Clouds slid back over the moon and darkness thickened. The fog grew flat and heavy. An acrid stink rose, sharp enough to sting her eyes. Wendy covered her nose and mouth with her sleeve and breathed through mud crusted cloth.

Trees rustled behind her.

She spun.

Nothing. Trunks. Shadows. Fog.

Quiet filled the world.

No laughing. No men talking. No crickets. No animals at all.

The mountain held its breath.

Had the hunters caught up?

Wendy lifted her chin. Her voice rose strong and steady through her softened throat. "I'm on the Path of Ascension. Do not interfere," she said.

Faith fortified the words from pleading to divine commandment.

Nothing answered.

Nothing could interfere in her quest for Ascension. This was her fate. She was chosen.

She started walking again—up, toward the next blue pulse.

Something cracked under her shoe.

Thin. Delicate. A fancy plate?

Wendy crouched and scraped mud aside with her fingers. White shards emerged from the muck—flat and smooth, with narrow slits where eyes would be. No mouth. No nose. Just blank.

A mask.

She fitted the pieces together in her lap. Mud crusted most of it, but where her thumb rubbed the surface clean, dark streaks showed through—dry crimson smeared along the cheeks.

Someone bloody had held this.

Wendy's breath caught. The prints—thin and small—clung close to the eye slits, as if someone had tried to claw it off. The way you would claw for eyes if you were desperate. The way Wendy would.

A gasp burst out of her.

This mask.

The faceless masks from her dream. *Her* faithful.

Impossible.

Her stomach folded, shivered with the familiarity of it – the déjà vu of something remembered yet never lived.

Dream…or memory?

Wendy flung the mask away.

A jagged shard ripped through her finger as it left her hand. Pain flashed bright and clean. Blood welled and dotted the mask's cheek where it landed in the mud, her red mixing with the older brown smear.

The mask stared up at her from the ground.

Wendy flicked off the welling blood and breathed slowly.

She wasn't the first one on this mountain.

This had happened before.

Did that woman survive?

Wendy's jaw locked. *I will.*

God had sent her that dream. God had shown her the mask. God had shown her Horn with the blade before she saw him in the shed. She'd known it before it happened, the way she'd known danger all her life before it spoke.

But in the dream, God was dead.

And the monsters had worn her face.

Wendy's mind tried to chase the questions down and pin them to the ground.

Why?

How?

What—

Questions. Always questions.

Questions got you punished.

Wendy swallowed the rest of her thoughts. Bitter. Too thick for her throat.

Footsteps were closing in. Breathing. Heavy, wet huffs. Growling.

Wendy listened.

Then—after a shift in the fog, after a soft press of something stepping where it shouldn't.

These weren't the men down the mountain.

But they were still part of Ascension. Another test. Another distraction meant to pull her off the path.

They wouldn't stop her.

Faith didn't make you invincible. Wendy knew that. Faith hadn't protected her when she crossed God. God didn't ask for understanding. He asked for obedience.

Now she stayed silent.

No questions about who's out there. No demanding an identity from her pursuers. No questions on the path.

Just up. Just the next light. Just the promise that Ascension would give her what she needed.

She took another sip of water, wiped the blood from her finger on her muddied suit, and kept climbing.

Behind her, the watchers followed—quiet and patient as Death.

SIX

The night stretched on.

Wendy dragged herself from tree to tree because her feet had stopped being feet. They were just anchors dragging behind her. Her shoes couldn't come out of the mud anymore—they slid through it with a wet rasp.

She tripped. Slicing her ankle on a rock.

"Shit," she cried.

And the mountain let that echo. Her voice rising up the slope, tumbling down it, without the fog's intervention.

She caught herself before falling on a tree.

Breathe through the pain, the kind voice said. A memory flashed. Bright white uniform. Thick yellow fabric tied around her waist. The man was examining her ankle. *Just a little sprain. You want to go on?* Wendy nodded. *Then just breathe through the pain.*

But there wasn't enough air here. Each breath was like sucking through an empty straw. The cold wasn't clean anymore. It had teeth. It burned her chest from the inside with every gasp.

She pushed herself forward, climbing, feet slipping into the rocks as she moved upward.

Fog pressed close. Hiding the stones broke through the ground like knuckles.

Don't fall.

Don't fall.

If she went down on those rocks, her bones would break like sticks. Her face would split like her ankle, painting the mountain with her dark red blood. She would lie there, heat washing out of her, and listen as the mountain finished her.

With what? Wild animals eating her alive? A mud slide drowning her? Or the long glare of Death sitting atop a stone, watching her wither away?

Wendy didn't let herself picture it.

She only kept moving.

Ascension meant up.

Up meant staying alive.

Behind her, the mountain groaned.

Snaps. Crunches. Deadfall breaking under weight. The sound came from everywhere at once, circling, closing.

The men had gone quiet. No more joking. No more sports talk. Killing time now. The kind of quiet Wendy knew from dark cars right before a hand grabbed your wrist. Quiet when you thought he fell asleep and you could slip away, but then he asks where you're going.

Wendy flexed her fingers, curling them into claws. If they wanted killing time, she'd show them what that meant.

Then her stomach rolled. The shakes stuttered through her thighs. Her body was still her body—thin and empty and full of buzzing.

A growl rose in the fog.

Then another.

Then another.

She smiled anticipating their screams.

Their pleading for her to stop.

Their cries for their mothers to save them before they understood there was no salvation from her.

She was the agent of God.

Wendy kept her eyes ahead, searching for the next blue light. No pulse. No blue.

"I am on the Path," she rasped, voice raw. "Ascension."

She hugged a tree for two breaths, one palm pressed hard to bark, then shoved herself forward again.

When she stopped, the sounds stopped.

They weren't rushing her.

They were letting the mountain do the work.

Let her exhaust herself. Let her fall.

They didn't know her.

They didn't know what the Sleep House had made.

A memory slammed through her like lightning.

Cassie.

Cassie burst through the Sleep House entrance, her brother—if that's what he was—shoving her forward. Her light filled the foyer. He accepted something from one of the basement people. They were waiting for his arrival – standing at the basement entrance just beyond the gloom. Something changed hands. Fast. Like it didn't matter. The man pushed Cassie toward the basement.

Cassie screamed.

The basement dweller answered with a wet, slobbering laugh, drool slid over his gray, sore-crusted lips.

Cassie whimpered. The man dragged her toward the basement door.

Wendy had to save her light.

Needed it.

Wendy lunged. Nails to face. Popping the basement dweller's eyes. A kick. He tumbled down the stairs, bones snapping, darkness swallowing his shrieks.

Others reached from the corners—hands and mouths hungry for Cassie's glow.

Wendy tore through them in a frenzy. She didn't feel their claws and teeth breaking her skin. She only felt Cassie behind her, bright and shaking and alive.

When the stairs ran black with Basement Dweller blood, the few remaining retreated, leaving only Wendy and Cassie's light.

Wendy carried Cassie to the safety of the library —where no one would kill Cassie's light.

No one but Wendy.

The memory's thunder awoke her muscles, her lungs, her soul. She climbed faster, riding the thunder of it before it faded.

The air here, the little there was, revived her. She'd breathed the Sleep House rot too long. The mold in the basement, the mildew dripping from the windows, the faithful who didn't bathe, didn't bother to get off the floor to relieve themselves, just wallowed in their filth—like her.

"Just a taste," a voice hissed.

Wendy jerked. The words slapping her.

Disgust dripped from those words. The man who said them knew she was trash. Knew her as the sinner she proved to be, the murderer.

She stumbled.

Her boot slipped through the mud.

She fell. Hard.

Her chin struck stone. Pain flashed white. Blood burst hot down her throat.

From the edge of the fog, the owner of that horrid voice stepped into being.

He was large—too large. Fog curled greedily around him, dragging his black trench coat into the night's deep emptiness. It was impossible to tell where the night ended and the man began—but he stepped toward Wendy, pulling away from the night. Under the deep shadows of his hood: a pale glimmer.

A white mask.

Blank.

Watching.

Her stomach dropped.

A scream whimpered out of her.

The mask was like the one she'd found down the mountain—mud-caked, smeared with old blood.

This was one of them.

One of the hunters—

Wendy snarled and scrambled backward, keeping her face toward it. Her hands found rocks. Her nails dug in.

"Just a taste," the mask man said.

He held something out.

Even in this fog, this suffocating dark, Wendy knew it.

A baggie.

Grace.

Not God's white Grace – this was toxic waste brown. The kind of drugs she knew from before the Sleep House.

Her mouth flooded. Her whole body leaned toward it. Want knifed through her—an ecstatic sound slipping out.

God, she wanted it.

Just a taste would quiet the quivering under her skin. Just a taste would help her breathe. Would make the cold stop biting. Would make her chest stop burning.

Just a taste might be okay.

It wasn't much.

Her hand lifted.

The masked man stretched closer, offering it like a gift. Black smoke billowed around him turning the fog into starless night sky.

Wendy's fingers brushed the smooth, filthy plastic.

Then God's voice rose in her head—slick and familiar, the way it always sounded when He wanted her to remember her place.

Do you remember the sins that put you here? I do.

Wendy froze.

A test.

A Tempter.

If she took this, she fell—off the Path, out of Ascension, back into the pit.

"Tempter," Wendy spat.

She slapped the baggie into the fog.

The man roared behind the mouthless mask—animal rage trapped in blank porcelain.

She shoved herself away, scrambling over rocks, and ran up the mountain.

"Just a taste," the thing hissed. "Just a—"

The voice cut off.

Something wet and choking followed—gargling, strangled—then silence.

Wendy didn't look back.

She ran blind up the slope, lungs seizing, legs numb, hands slapping trees to keep her from going down. "I'm on the path," Wendy gasped. "Ascension!"

"Just a taste," another voice whispered ahead.

Then another.

Then three at once—hissing from trunks, from the ground, from the fog itself.

Their breath steamed against her cheeks. Their stink rolled in—humid and foul, the same acrid rot she'd smelled earlier, thick enough to press tears from her eyes.

Not bears.

Not wolves.

People weren't the only hunters on this mountain.

Their voices climbed to shrieks swallowing the world beyond the fog and moonlight.

Wendy ran.

Mud sprayed from her feet. Her arms flailed to keep balance. She bounced off trees, grabbed bark, shoved herself forward. Her suit, faintly glowing under its mud, made her a moving target in the fog.

The masked men kept pace without touching her.

They swarmed the trees. Claws scraped bark. Wood curls rained down. Shapes leapt branch to branch and screamed in her ear, always the same words in shifting voices.

"Just a taste."

"Taste it."

No blue. Only fog and her own ragged breathing.

Her mind emptied down to one hard command: up.

A yelp broke the chorus behind her.

Then another.

Something was grabbing them. Choking them the way the first voice had cut off.

Wendy didn't slow.

This was temptation. This was Scripture with teeth. She wouldn't falter. Not now.

A figure ran past her in the fog—human-sized, moving clean. Clothes like Horn's.

Wendy veered away, reflexes as sharp as pain. The man held a pole ending in a hoop—metal, round, the kind you used to catch and drag dogs.

Not for her, she realized as he extended it into the fog beside her, snagging something Wendy couldn't see.

A hiss. A sizzle. Burnt plastic smell hit her nose.

The thing screamed.

Wendy kept running.

Another blue light pulsed ahead—weak through fog, a wound in the dark.

She locked onto it.

Lungs were iron. Muscles were stone. Survival screamed: you stop, you die.

Death would be easy. All she had to do was stop. All she had to do was take what was offered. What she wanted…needed.

But dying as this—a discarded thing left on a mountain—was worse. Worse than death. Worse than the basement. Worse than being nothing. This was dying at the door of God's plan…too weak to crawl through…to become who she is meant to be.

"Tempters!" she rasped. "Tempters! I'm on the Path!"

Blue light bled through the fog, a pulsing wound in the darkness.

Someone stood beside it—still and waiting. Their shadow stretched too long, swallowing the path, draping her in its darkness as she ascended.

"Just a taste!"

"Taste it!"

"No!" Wendy's voice tore. Her heart hammered to break from her chest, to splinter bone, to release the growth within her. "No!"

A shape lunged out of the fog.

Wendy's hand hit his white mask.

Cold smoothness under her palm.

A black cloak wrapped around the space beside her, close enough that she smelled wet smoke.

A bony hand shoved a baggie of brown powder into her face.

Her legs gave.

She clawed upward anyway, ripping at the mask like a reflex, like the woman from the mountain, like Wendy had always done—go for the eyes, go for the face, blind the thing that wants you.

The mask tore free.

Underneath: not a man.

Skin black as a starless sky. Eyes burning red. Horns thrusting from its forehead.

Wendy forgot how to breathe. Her head swam as every nerve in her quaked, not from dope sickness, but from the déjà vu hammering her mind.

This thing was the faithful from her dream.

Real.

Here.

Black smoke poured off its face and cloak, swallowing the fog's gray with a deeper night. It reached for its mask—panicked, fumbling—like it needed the lie to breathe.

A hoop snapped around its neck.

The cowboy yanked.

The creature screamed. Flesh sizzled. The air reeked with burnt plastic and toxic brown smoke.

It hit the ground hard, thrashing.

Wendy didn't wait to see more.

She crawled. Clawed. Sinking her nails through the muddy earth, pulling herself to the blue light. There was nothing left in the world.

Only the light.

And the man in the light.

Other voices hissed behind her, offering. Pleading. Dying off one by one as something choked them into silence.

Wendy's mouth opened in silent prayer as she pulled herself into the bubble of blue glow.

Silence fell.

Only her panting remained. Her hands scraping. Her knees sliding. Her growl low in her throat.

God said to show her faith. She dug deeper into the earth to pull, but she couldn't pull her face from the mud. She dragged it through the muck, her arms no longer under her control but fueled with the faith God had in her completing Ascension. He knew she could do it. He knew.

Her fingers pulled no more when her skin felt the light. She rolled her head. Seeing it – seeing him.

Every bone spent.

Every muscle empty.

The figure knelt.

A face leaned into the fog, lit by the pulsing blue.

A wide smile that didn't reach his eyes.

Horn.

He offered Wendy his hand.

The light hummed—an insect sound, steady and electric. Warning or invitation. Wendy couldn't tell. Wendy couldn't care. Her mind searched for God's answer and found only the taste of blood and smoke.

Her breath stuttered.

Where was the certainty?

Where was the command?

Horn's palm waited—open, empty.

Wendy's hand twitched. Her skin itched. Her fingers curled.

No. Don't, the growth in her growled. It throbbed harder than her heart. *Leave the light. Run.*

Her hand fell into his, unable to hold it up anymore.

His grip was warm. Human.

Her skin crawled—like her body knew what her faith refused to see.

SEVEN

Horn eased Wendy onto an air mattress. It squeaked under her slight weight. Clean flannel sheets were pulled taut. No stains. No dark smears. Nothing like what she had for years.

She lay numb, running her fingertips over the fabric, slow, like touch could prove this was real. The sheets were warm. They smelled like the mountain—wet earth and sap—and something sharp and clean she couldn't name. Chemical. Bright. Like cleanliness itself had a scent.

"You made it," Horn said. "Few do."

Wendy's head rolled toward his voice. The rest of her refused to follow. She tried to ask what he was doing, but her tongue was too big for her mouth, unable to form words. So, she just mumbled.

Horn moved with the same controlled focus he'd shown in the shed—no wasted motion, no softness. He didn't hover over her. He didn't look for gratitude. He just built camp like it was a job that kept someone alive.

Rain clung to his mustache. His breath came hard, engine-steady, steaming into the cold air.

"Water." He set a metal bottle in one hand. "Protein drink." A plastic bottle in the other. "And if your stomach can handle it—a banana. It'll help with cramps."

Wendy didn't move.

Horn rolled her onto her side like she weighed nothing. When her hands couldn't lift the bottles, he sat her up and braced her against his chest, firm and careful. He raised the water to her lips.

Wendy took a long pull—too much, too fast.

"Whoa." Horn lowered the bottle with a soft chuckle. "Slow. You'll get sick, and the medicine needs to stay in your stomach."

Wendy nodded. Air scraped in and out of her throat. Her chest loosened enough to pull air deeper.

Horn laid her back down on her side again, patted her shoulder once—an odd, brief touch—and moved to a patch of mud facing her.

He watched her like a live wire. Not hungry. Not slimy. Cautious.

Wendy watched him back.

He held a cotton ball and a square brown bottle. "Can I clean your ankle? Already looks angry – probably infected."

She didn't move.

He pressed the cotton to the bottle, tipped it, and then pressed the wet swab to her ankle. She didn't feel the burn through the rest of her screaming body.

When she didn't react, he moved faster. Finally applying a band-aid and moving away.

Kindness was just another tool people used to get you off balance. So was calm. So was patience.

God trusted Horn with Ascension.

That didn't mean Wendy should.

He moved about the small campsite, packing away his first aid kit and taking out a canteen for himself. He sipped, watching her.

Wendy took a few more measured sips of her own water. After some of the white drink, she sat up without the room tilting.

Horn drew in a deep breath, steam pouring out as he spoke. "Now you have a choice." His voice didn't rise. It didn't sermon. It landed flat and heavy. "Mr. Dream—the man who owns the Sleep House—thinks you're dead. No one, that I know of, has returned to him after Ascension."

Wendy's stomach tightened at the name. Mr. Dream. Not God. Horn wanted the name to feel smaller.

Another test.

"You can go back now if you want," Horn continued. "Ascension isn't complete, but I'll tell him you completed it. You'll return to your old life."

Old life…

Mold. Moans. Darkness. The constant hint of Grace drifting through the air. The numbness…the nothing it brought.

"Or," Horn continued, "you can stay with me on this mountain, become an Aspirant, and face the hardest trial of Ascension. The few who have made it this far, only two – that I have seen – have ever completed what comes next. But by completing Ascension, you will become a new person. Your soul can start again."

Only two?

She wasn't finished?

Wendy stared past him into the fog.

Down the mountain: darkness and voices, the smell of hunters.

Up the mountain: gray mist and…what?

She wasn't at the top. She wasn't back at the bottom. She was somewhere in-between, and she couldn't stay there. At some point, you had to move. Up or down, she had to do something otherwise, she might as well lay back under the stairs.

You made it. Few do.

What happened to those who failed Ascension? Did the Tempters take them? Did they simply die on the spot?

She sipped the water, following its chill down her throat as it plummeted into her stomach. It landed heavy in her belly, reminding her that her body was empty.

Horn held up two glossy stones, one black, one white.

He shook the black one, "Stay."

He shook the white one, "Go." Then placed them beside her. "Hand me the one you want."

Wendy stared at them.

God knew she was not dead.

Horn is offering a way back without finishing.

Which meant Horn could lie to Mr. Dream.

Which meant Horn could lie to her.

And if she returns without completing Ascension, if God didn't believe Horn's story, she'd be cast from the Sleep House—a failure. Never again welcomed back to Grace.

And then what?

There was nothing but demons beyond the Sleep House. Death, as Cassie knew, was the only escape.

Cassie lost her faith. Then lost her life.

There was no decision to be made.

Another test of her faith.

Both stones were impossibly heavy. But she pushed the black stone across the mud toward Horn.

Horn watched it slide. His expression unchanged, but something in him settled—as if he'd been waiting for exactly this.

The black stone throbbed in the pulsing blue camp light. It beat like a heart out of rhythm with the world.

Horn turned out the light.

Darkness swallowed them.

"Get some sleep," Horn said. "Your mind, body, and soul need rest. We start our climb in the morning."

Wendy's body sank into the mattress like it wanted to disappear. If Horn attacked her now, she couldn't stop it. If he waited until she slept, she couldn't stop that either.

But he didn't come close.

Wendy kept her eyes open until the dark softened and her pupils did what the Sleep House had trained them to do. The world didn't go black for her the way it did for other people. Edges remained. Shapes held.

She could see the outline of Horn's face.

Horn sat where he was, pulled a beaded bracelet off his wrist, and began sliding the beads through his fingers. His lips moved. Only steam came out.

Another figure emerged from the fog—same shape of cloak, smaller body, younger movements.

Wendy tensed. Her muscles tried to remember violence. They remembered nothing.

The younger man stopped a few paces away and said to Horn, "Brother, we secured thirty-one."

"Thirty-one?" Horn's head turned. In the dim, Wendy saw his profile tighten, worry mixed with fear. He caught himself from looking at her. "Nice work. Request reinforcements for tomorrow." He let out a long breath. "I don't want any surprises during the next phase." Then, sharper: "Dismissed, Acolyte— and remember, I'm not a brother yet."

The younger man laughed. "I'm sure it will be imminent," he said.

His voice faded down the mountain.

Laughter from the other men rose from downslope. The joyous noise moved away.

"They don't want my kind in the Brotherhood," Horn grumbled to no one. "They want college kids, not people forged by faith."

He stared up the mountain for a long moment.

Horn opened a sleeping bag, then brought her some heavy blankets. They were soft and thick and warm. He draped them over her like Wendy imagined a loving parent would do a child.

Horn climbed into his sleeping bag. He sat upright, still working the beads through his fingers. His whispered words joined the fog as puffs of white steam.

Praying.

Sharing secrets with the mountain.

The sight tugged something loose in Wendy.

A memory—old, blurred at the edges. Not her mother. A man's voice, the voice she heard earlier, kind and gentle. A room that smelled like soap. Wendy as a child, hands folded wrong, trying anyway.

Her mom had been furious. *God never helped no one*, she'd snapped.

And the man had answered, gentle as if he wasn't afraid of her mother at all: *God helps us every day—we just can't see it.*

Wendy stared at Horn's moving lips.

In the Sleep House, was God helping?

God came down from the heavens to punish. God tossed Grace like feed. His servants brought the trashcans of food. His servants filled the water bowls.

Help.

The word tasted strange.

Wendy tried to stay awake. She tried to keep watch.

But exhaustion settled with the fog.

Her eyes closed.

No dreams came.

85

EIGHT

Cold slapped Wendy across the face.

She screamed and sprang upright, lungs seizing. Water sheeted down her cheeks, soaked her collar, ran icy fingers under the jumpsuit. For a second her body forgot soreness. Forgot exhaustion. All she had was shock—pure, bright, alive.

Horn stood a few feet away with an empty bucket.

"Morning sunshine," he said and smiled.

Wendy's hands curled into claws.

"Sorry," Horn tossed her a towel. "You weren't waking up – and I didn't want to get in arm's reach." He smiled to hide his hesitation, as if to say *I know better.*

Wendy wiped her face, the towel rough on her skin. Her heart hammered, shaking her ribs. Cold water trickled over her lips. She licked at them absently.

The fog had thinned. Gray clouds bulged low over the mountain, heavy as wet blankets. The trees around them were stripped down to skeletal limbs, bark split and bleeding sap. The air smelled sweet and raw, mixed with damp earth. It was clean in a way that made Wendy's chest ache.

Was it this clean last night?

"How are you feeling?" Horn asked.

Lighter.

She wiggled her toes, rolled her ankles, flexed her legs. Yes. Lighter was right. Anchors cut free. As if she could float away.

He set a glass of water and another protein drink on the ground near her feet—close enough to reach, not close enough for his hands to be in range. "Breakfast."

Wendy picked up the water and sniffed it. She drank slowly. The protein drink was chalky—thick like the vanilla from last night, but without the comfort.

Horn watched her swallow. "Any sickness?"

Wendy shook her head.

"Good," he said. "Finish up and we'll be on our way. We've got a lot of ground to cover before tonight."

Horn went to a stuffed backpack and rummaged through it, shoving a large canteen into his cloak's pocket. Rope hung from the side of the pack, think and rough. She waited for him to throw it, demand she tie herself up, to be easier to control.

But he didn't.

He stretched his back. It didn't pop. He groaned as he looked up the mountain.

Rain fell in gray curtains up there. It streaked down from the heavens like long fingers reaching, grabbing, searching for her.

The climb ahead was steep, sheer in places, and hidden by clouds.

"What's up there?" she asked.

"Another choice. Maybe your last choice, Aspirant." Horn shrugged. "We'll see."

Ascension, Wendy thought. The word had teeth now. It wasn't a sermon anymore — it was a climb, a punishment, a game with rules only other people knew.

Horn was worried.

And that worried Wendy most of all.

God's uncertainty yesterday.

Horn's uncertainty now.

Did anyone know anything?

Horn carried himself like a man who could fight. Calm. Certain. Built for violence the way some people were built for running, or sneaking.

Wendy felt the old instinct rise—memories blurred but sharp at the edges: dangerous men, rides she hadn't chosen, rooms smelling of boiling heroin and sex, her body always knew how to get out alive.

Faith carried her through those nights, or maybe stubbornness had. Either way, she was still here.

"Are you going to let me leave the mountain?" Wendy asked.

"No," Horn answered without looking at her. He was rolling his sleeping bag. "Who you are today will never leave this place." He grunted as he cinched the straps, his hands steady. "If you survive, you'll be someone else. Last night you could have left as who you were. That time's over."

Wendy nodded like she understood. Understanding didn't matter. Only survival mattered.

She said, "God will give me what I need to survive."

Horn gave a small sound—agreement or dismissal, Wendy couldn't tell. "No one weak in faith survives Ascension," he said. Then his gaze drifted down the mountain as if he could see something that wasn't there. "But faith isn't always a gift." His voice went quieter. "Not everyone values it. Not anymore."

Sadness swept over Horn. His stare drifted back to a past Wendy couldn't imagine. Their lives had been different, but Wendy knew listless dreaming when she saw it. Better days danced behind Horn's blank stare.

Wendy had learned not to ask. She simply stood and pulled the blankets from her bed.

Horn held up a hand.

"Leave your mattress. Last night was your last night for comfort," he said. His eyes met hers. "My acolytes will come for it after we leave."

Acolytes.

Thirty-one.

Reinforcements…

The words sat in Wendy's mouth like muddy grit.

She nodded again.

And in that moment, she felt it—pressure in the air that wasn't fog. Presence. Eyes. Not just Horn's. More. Too many to count.

The mountain? Was it watching her?

Wendy's breath tightened.

She scanned the cleared slope, the stripped trees, the wet rocks. Nothing moved. No bodies. No footsteps. Only the hush of the mountain waiting.

But she felt them anyway.

Around her.

Behind her.

Inside the spaces between trees.

Last night she'd been hunted.

Now she was being herded.

Wendy's jaw set. Her fists clenched. She pulled a sharp breath into her lungs and held it like a weapon.

Helpless? Never.

"Let's go," Horn said. "Follow me. Don't stray from the path, and don't fall too far behind."

She didn't ask why.

The answer surrounded her. The hunt was over. Now the march to death began. Beyond the fog, beyond the clouds, the mountain silently held Horn's secrets. They climbed into that silence, not looking back, ascending steadily toward their destination.

He'll kill you up there, the growth inside her said.

Wendy didn't argue.

NINE

The sun was a weak, swollen smear behind the fog—more bruise than light—when Wendy and Horn finally broke above the worst of the fog.

Wendy panted heavily, struggling to keep pace with Horn.

He wasn't even winded.

Ice crystals clung to his beard. Every so often he chuckled, delighted, and flicked them out with two fingers like he was brushing away glitter. Under his brown cloak he wore jeans and heavy hiking boots—real boots, made for mountains, made for moving.

Wendy's jumpsuit had been white once. Now it was a skin of mud and grass stains with a gash on her knee from where she'd fallen. The fabric held cold against her like it remembered Horn's bucket, like it wanted to keep punishing her.

The mountain joined in on the punishment. It didn't care about her faith. It didn't reward effort. Mud slicks stole her footing with each step. Horn held steady. He moved through deadfall like the forest opened for him. Wendy clumsily tumbled over the same logs, catching herself on bark and stone, teeth bared, breath ragged.

"Can you slow down?" she gasped, almost falling over a slick root. "I'm not dressed for this."

Horn didn't slow. He glanced back, with an easy smile. "You think my clothes make my climb easier?"

Wendy's foot slid out. She hit the forest floor with a wet squelch. Mud slapped her face. She growled and pushed up to her knees, shaking with anger. She flung her hand at his boots. "Yeah. You've got those. My shoes keep slipping and they're soaked through."

Horn stopped.

He didn't mock her.

He looked down at Wendy's feet like he was actually measuring the problem. Then he sat on the nearest rock and unlaced his boots.

When he held them out, Wendy stared.

This had '*trap*' written all over it. A kindness offered too neatly. The moment where she reached, her wrist would be snatched in his rough grip. Twisted. Broken to teach her he'd never give her anything for free.

But Horn just waited.

Smiling.

Boots in hand. Calm. Patient. Like the mountain had taught him how to wait people out.

Wendy's throat worked. "Why?"

Horn shrugged. "Because you'll break your ankle in those shoes, and then you're dead weight." He said it like it was a fact, not an insult. "You need to be able to walk when we get where we're going."

Need.

The word snagged in Wendy's mind.

Not *want*. Not *should*. Need.

Wendy looked at his socked feet—threadbare, wet already, toes pressing into mud like he didn't care if the cold bit him.

"Is this a joke to you," she said.

Horn, expressionless, said, "Nothing about you is funny."

Wendy didn't know whether that was respect or warning.

She carefully took the boots.

They were heavy. Too heavy. The weight alone felt like a prank. Her legs were already burning—ripping boots like these from sucking mud would turn every step into a punishment.

Her mother's voice rose in her head, spiteful and bright: *You get what you deserve.*

Wendy swallowed and forced herself upright.

Horn watched her wrestle her feet into the boots. "But you are interesting. You notice everything," he said casually, like he was talking about weather. "Like when you were counting voices in the van."

Wendy's head snapped up. "How—"

Horn shrugged. "It's my duty to notice what you notice."

Wendy's skin tightened. Duty made her think of ledgers and cages. Trades and bargains. Cassie and her *brother*.

"You kept your head," Horn continued. "You didn't beg. You didn't bargain. You didn't take the taste when it was offered. Most do."

Wendy's stomach clenched. The word *taste* still had teeth.

Horn leaned forward slightly, turning his attention to a weight bearing down on Wendy. "Do you know what the Sylvan Order calls that?"

Wendy didn't answer. Silence was safer.

Horn didn't seem bothered. "Discipline," he said. "It's rarer than faith. But faith is getting rarer by the day."

Sylvan Order.

Wendy let the words settle in her mouth like grit. "Brotherhood," she said carefully. "That's what your *acolyte* called it."

Horn's jaw tightened. Just a flicker. "No. He called me a brother. I'm simply an acolyte like them."

"Then, what is the Sylvan Order? A cult?" Wendy asked, then immediately regretted it. Questions got you punished.

Horn studied her. Had Wendy just extended her throat?

Presenting it for his blade.

That curved blade, the growth in her chuckled.

"Not a cult. A structure," he said. "A set of vows. A way of keeping what lives up here contained." He paused. "And a way to take back what is rightfully ours."

Wendy's flesh prickled, turning cold. "What is *ours?*"

Horn motioned to her feet. She was done tying his boots but remained seated on the rocks.

"Ours, as in each of ours, not as in mine. We own our souls. The Order helps people remember to reclaim them when they give them away."

Wendy's heart hammered. "To God?"

Horn's expression didn't change, but something behind his eyes shut a door. "Mr. Dream. Names matter. He's a man, not a God. That's why I don't let my acolytes call me Brother."

"Then say his name," Wendy said. "If he's only a man," she pressed, "say it."

A beat of silence passed—thin, telling.

Horn's jaw tightened. "Noah. Now, keep walking. We have a time limit here."

Noah?

God. Mr. Dream. Now, Noah.

Was he only a man after all?

Wendy's gaze narrowed. "So, what am I?"

Horn's boots were biting into her calves now. Heavy. Unforgiving. She shifted her weight, fighting a tremor.

Horn nodded at her discomfort like he'd expected it. "An Aspirant, maybe," he said. "Or a sacrifice. Or…" His mouth twitched again, almost reluctant. "Or bait."

Bait.

That word hit Wendy harder than *discipline*.

"So, which is it?" she said.

Horn didn't deny it. "The mountain will reveal your true self," he said. "The mountain devours most people. The Sleep House makes ghosts. You…" His gaze held her—steady, assessing. "You are still deciding."

Wendy's ribs tightened. The growth within pulsed, burned.

Horn's voice became quieter. "You think you're being marched to your death."

Wendy didn't blink. "I'm the Sacrifice."

Horn held her stare. "That's to be seen," he said.

"And those who survive?" Wendy asked before she could stop herself. "You said you've seen two survive."

Horn smiled without warmth. "No more questions."

Wendy's stomach dropped.

There was something beyond Ascension.

What?

She forced her feet to move. The heavy boots sank into the mountain deeper than her shoes ever had. She yanked them free with a grunt.

Horn started walking again. Mud swallowed his socks with every step.

A tremor ran through Wendy—withdrawal, cold, fear, all braided together.

"How much farther?" she asked, voice tighter now. Not pleading. Calculating.

Horn stopped when he heard the edge in it. "You're shaking," he said. "Break. One minute. And I said no more questions."

He dropped his pack on a rock and dug through it. Horn pulled out an orange bottle. He shook out two white pills and offered them with his small canteen.

Wendy took the pills. Paused at the canteen. "What's in this?"

Horn sighed exasperated, "Water."

Wendy swallowed, washing the pills down.

"You asked what was in the canteen but not the pills?" Horn said. He chuckled.

Wendy shrugged. "Looked like the ones from before."

"And you didn't question those either."

Wendy's eyes narrowed. "I trusted that you want me alive."

Horn's smile returned—small, sharp.

Rain broke from the sky in sudden sheets. It hit branches, hammered leaves, dripping in heavy rhythms around them. The fog thickened again, swallowing distance.

Wendy looked upslope through the rain.

Deep ahead, a muted gold light flickered through the wet gray—steady, human-made. A campfire, maybe. A lantern. Something waiting.

"There," Horn said.

Wendy stared at the light and felt something in her shift— not hope, not relief.

Dread.

The dread of realizing there were rooms inside this mountain, and rules inside the rooms, and people who believed they owned the climb.

She pressed on.

Not because she trusted Horn.

Because she needed to see the light. To see what was inside.

TEN

Twilight bled across the horizon as they reached the cave.

The grumbling generator announced itself long before Wendy saw it. In the mountain's silence, the engine's chug filled everything. Steady. Blunt. Mechanical. It drowned the forest in sound.

Steel poles were scattered around the cave mouth, each topped with harsh electric lights. Thick black cables ran from them like entrails, coiling and converging at the generator. This was a makeshift campsite, set up quickly and ready to be torn down just as fast.

Inside, the cave walls were golden with shimmering flecks. They caught the light like diamonds, sparkling a beautiful invitation for Wendy to enter.

Wendy kept her mouth shut. Habit. Questions got punished.

She looked at Horn anyway—once, quick—testing for permission.

Horn invited the question with a wave of his hand.

"What's in the wall?" Wendy shouted over the generator.

"Mica." He put his pack on a table near the generator and continued, "Well, technically this is known as muscovite, and it's pretty common around here."

He glanced at the glittering wall and smirked. "It looks magical."

Wendy stared at the flecks. Her mouth tightened.

Nothing was magic.

She'd believed in miracles in the Sleep House—because everyone else did, because disbelief got you punished, because you needed something bigger than yourself when life was nothing but hunger and rot.

With a clear mind she could finally see the truth: God's miracles had been tricks—hidden bulbs, men with spotlights. She'd seen the wires after.

Why would God need tricks to prove his divinity? Wendy didn't permit an answer to fester from this question and instead, moved into the cave.

"And it'll lie to you about light," he added. "Don't think you can follow reflections out. People try. They get turned around."

There was a tunnel. Black. Clean edges. Unnatural edges. More chiseled by man than nature.

Over the tunnel was a carving, a relief: a man strapped to a table, ribs and throat exposed in stylized lines. Another figure leaned over him, hooded, robed, broad – like Horn. Something was being pulled out of the man on the table, a twisting coil, spiraling up. The man was ripping out the spiral…the spiral, Wendy repeated the word in her mind feeling it slip over her soul slick and greasy.

Spiral.

Spiral.

The Spiral.

"Is this why I'm here?" Wendy pointed to the carving without taking her eyes from it.

"Yep." Horn took the canteen from his bag and gave it to her. "Still just water." He handed her another protein drink. "Hungry?"

She shook her head. "Is that like, a human sacrifice or something?"

"Or something." Horn got his own water and took a long drink. Beads of water dribbled over his beard.

The tunnel swallowed the light as the mountain's fog swallowed sound. Beyond the entrance, the tunnel's darkness was absolute. It was the darkness of the Sleep House basement. And, as with the Sleep House, Death dwelled within.

"Who made this place?" The relief sculpture. The tunnel. The lights. The generator. Someone prepared this place.

Who?

Horn didn't answer with words.

He turned away from her and unzipped a smaller leather satchel from inside his pack. The bag was stuffed full. A long handle protruded from it—metal gleaming cold even under electric light.

A knife.

Wendy's throat tightened. Everything in her narrowed to that shine.

"Why bring me here for this?" Her voice came sharp, thin. Within her the sickness was building. It had been throughout the day. The higher they went, the sicker she became – and not simply dope sick but something deeper.

The mountain drained her.

Reduced her to exhaustion as she battled the mud, as she struggled to breathe the little air there was, as she pressed through the drenching rain.

He drove her here. No rest. No breath. No mercy. So, she couldn't fight.

She slowly backed away. Her hand found the ice-cold stone wall, her heel striking the wall.

Did Horn bring her here to rip the spiral from her? The coiling, growing, throbbing thing that pulled her toward the tunnel.

Go. Run in there and I'll find you, the growth said as it burned.

There was nowhere to go. That was his cave. His tunnel. Whoever made it, Horn used it. He brought others here.

How many bodies were tossed in there?

Her hot, heavy breath fogged in the freezing mountain air.

Beyond the cave mouth was nothing but darkness. No distant city lights. No cars. No planes. Only the night. A darkness she lived within for so long – she had forgotten mountains, trees, sky. All the things the mountain showed her through the morning and day. There was more than darkness here – more than darkness out there.

Out there was a world she didn't remember. A life she hadn't lived—and now she'd lose the rest of that life.

Dying without living—was there a worse fate?

Fight or flight awoke in her.

Something in Wendy's ribs stirred, pleased by her fear. It cackled. Delighted in her horror. The growth coiled, uncoiled.

Then another voice rose—older, gentler, sharp with love.

Firecracker.

The name struck through her like lightning.

For a second she saw a man's hands—big, careful—showing her how to stand, how to plant her feet, how to throw weight into a punch. A voice saying again but not cruel. A voice saying, *you've got this*.

It was the man from before. The voice she's heard telling her to keep going on the mountain.

Yacob.

Her stepdad.

The one person who had loved her without making her pay for it.

His name hurt like dull fingers digging into a bruise.

Her eyes burned. She swallowed hard, forcing herself to breathe.

How could she forget him? The only good man she's ever known. How could she forget *him?*

This God damn mountain! It forced itself on her. Forced her to breathe the forest air instead of the stale toxins of the Sleep House. It exhausted her body in the light instead of letting her die motionless in the dark. Worst of all it stole the haze of memories from her life and replaced them with nightmarish clarity. The fog of her childhood was breaking over the mountain. Wendy shivered at the horrors this place would unveil. They were coming. And she whimpered hoping the fog would conceal them forever more.

Horn shoved the satchel toward her.

Wendy flinched away. She yelped.

He pulled it back, setting it down at her feet. "You'll need this in there," Horn said. He backed away slowly, cautiously giving Wendy space as she shivered against the stone wall.

He said calmly, reassuringly, "I'm not here to hurt you." Then added, "But to be clear, I'm not here to save you either."

Wendy relaxed, fleeing the memories of Yacob. Returning to Horn and this place of sacrifice. She stared at him.

He pointed at the tunnel with two fingers. "Time gets weird. People go in for an hour and come out days later. Don't go off the path. You've got a few days' worth of supplies." He pointed at the satchel at her feet. "Go deep enough and you'll find a room. In that room, you can finish your Ascension ritual. Then you're done."

"If I survive?" She looked back at the carving above the door.

"If you survive," Horn agreed. "Then, I'll take you wherever you want to go."

Wendy's eyes settled again on the relief sculpture. The Spiral being pulled out like it was an organ.

"Ascension requires sacrifice," Horn said. Here it was, the sermon without the sanctimonious. Without the care or hope for her to be saved. This wasn't about salvation. It was about trial.

It was a crucible. "Not everyone is ready to give what's required. If you are not, then you will be taken by the mountain."

Horn returned to his pack and took out his sleeping bag. He unrolled it, taking care to prepare his bedding for a relaxing evening.

"There's a lantern just inside the cave," he said. "Matches are in the satchel. Fuel too. I'll be here when you're done." He glanced toward the sky. Rain pattered harder. "I'll be here a few days. So don't dally."

Wendy turned to the tunnel. The blackness beyond the cave's light was absolute. In the cave, the lights buzzed harsh warnings, don't go in there, beware…

"What's in there?" she asked.

The Path of Ascension led to darkness. From darkness the path began and in darkness the path shall end.

"You'll find your inner demons," Horn said. "If you've been hiding from something, it's down there. If you are afraid of something, it's in there. If you regret something, it will find you."

He rummaged in his bag, then brightened, finding his treasure. A thick paperback appeared in his hands. He held it up like a trophy. "While you're in there, I'll be finding out what happens with Stu and Frannie. Don't call for help. I can't help you."

Wendy's mouth went dry, all the moisture given by the mountain stolen by the cave. "You can't…or you won't?"

Horn smiled. "Both."

He glanced toward the cave mouth and raised his voice. "My men are outside. They won't let you abandon your commitment."

Wendy's pulse kicked.

Horn shouted into the fog below the cave's ledge, "Acolytes—sound off."

"Yes, Acolyte Horn!" came back—dozens of voices, close enough to feel.

Wendy felt the mountain shift around her, danger moving from surviving the climb to surviving the numbers. The army Horn commanded. The men who'd keep her here until she did what they wanted her to do.

Horn returned to his book, flipping back to a dog-eared page. He settled comfortably in his sleeping bag.

Wendy stared at him. The absurd normalcy of it—reading by a cave while she walked into the dark—her skin crawled.

Would he follow her in? Hunt her through the tunnels? Is this where the real trial began?

Horn set the book down and reached toward the generator. "Best find that lantern and get moving. You've got supplies in the satchel. The knife is for whatever purpose you see fit."

Wendy crouched and opened the satchel with fingers that didn't want to work.

Inside: bottles of water, protein drinks, a bottle of pills, matches, lantern fuel, a notebook and pen—tools for measuring and remembering—and the knife: ornate, heavy, too beautiful for something meant to cut food.

"Two pills a day," Horn said. "No more."

Then he clicked off the generator.

The engine died with a last reluctant grumble, and sudden silence hit like pressure. The mountain stole all sounds again, casting Wendy into the silent dark.

The cave mouth became the only shape—black on black. Rain pattered outside, each drop amplified by the stone until it sounded like fingers tapping on a coffin lid.

The relief above the tunnel seemed deeper without light— the spiral darker, the man on the table more helpless.

Horn clicked on a small flashlight over his book.

Wendy stood with the satchel straps in her fist.

Her body wanted sleep. Every muscle begged for it. Her knees ached. Her calves trembled inside the heavy boots. Rest was a mercy.

Rest was also how you died.

She could feel the shape of it: one minute to sit, then

another, then the mountain finishing what it had started. She'd never stand again. Never descend into the tunnel. Never live the life that waited to begin.

She wouldn't have left the Sleep House if the mountain hadn't forced her out. She'd been content to rot in place because rotting was easy.

Now clarity had returned like a blade. It cut through her, carving away the haze of her past, exposing the bones of who she truly was.

The horrible truth of who you really are, the growth groaned within her. *Maybe a short rest. Just a moment's delay?*

But delay meant surrender.

And whatever grew within her, was no friend. It never was.

Wendy stepped into the tunnel.

God abhorred failure. If marching into the void was what was required, then she would march. She would come back into the light and prove she was worth more than the pit.

A lantern sat just inside, its glass dull in the dark. Wendy's eyes adjusted to what they'd been trained for: shadows, corners, blackness that hid teeth.

She lit the lantern. The flame bloomed small and stubborn, and the tunnel's stone drank the light.

Wendy inhaled.

The dark filled her lungs like an old friend.

Then she walked forward.

The Sleep House had been the darkest place Wendy had ever known—until the tunnel took her.

ELEVEN

The tunnel swallowed Wendy, pulling her deeper, tightening, twisting.

Even with her hollow frame, the stone walls squeezed her. Her shoulders scraped through, catching more than once on jagged rock.

Her jumpsuit no longer showed any signs of its previous luminosity. The cave's dirt covered every inch, caked into the threads. Black smoke stained her arm where she held the lantern.

Wendy lifted the lantern higher and stared ahead.

No forks. No side passages. The tunnel just kept going, bending out of sight, then bending again. When Horn said, *follow the path*, she assumed there'd be a marker, not just a single hallway leading deeper into the cave.

"Where is this place?" Wendy said.

There were no junction points.

Her voice startled her. It was bigger down here—too loud, too present. The cave was listening. In the Sleep House, she'd learned to keep her words inside. Words attracted attention.

Attention got you hurt. Under the stairs, silence had been a blanket. You spoke only when you had to: for Grace, for mercy, for a lie.

She hadn't spoken much since Cassie.

Cassie's face rose behind Wendy's eyes, mousy brown hair, that crooked grin like she'd found something funny in the middle of hell. Cassie had stayed close even after Wendy's sin, even when the Grace stopped coming and the Sleep House grew meaner. Cassie sang on the nights when they had nothing. Soft lullabies, off-key and earnest, trying to make the moldy air feel less like a coffin.

She'd remind Wendy that tomorrow would be another chance to make things right, to take her rightful place in the light. But tomorrow was always a day away for Wendy because to ask for forgiveness was to invite God's wrath.

The tunnel breathed colder. The lantern hissed faintly as Wendy walked, flame tugging at the thin air.

And then—faint at first, then clearer—Cassie's song threaded into the rock around her.

A lullaby. Rainbows and pleasant dreams. Flying from where you were to somewhere you weren't supposed to reach. A place where the Sleep House stayed small and far behind you, where your life wasn't on a floorboard but among stars.

Wendy's throat tightened.

"That can't be Cassie," she told the dark. "She died. I saw her die."

The next words surged forward—*I let her…*but her mouth refused them. Her stomach clenched, she doubled over, her head grazing against an outcropping of rock.

"Shit!"

The cave swallowed her scream as the fog devoured sound on the mountain. There was no echo.

The pain flared through her skull, releasing a different thought.

"What kind of God lets someone like Cassie die?"

The lantern flame wavered, flinching at the blasphemy.

Wendy swallowed, her spit too thick, too big to fit down the tight space. Old powder, old bile, guilt that wouldn't dissolve lined her throat in jagged stone.

Cassie had run into the road. A car hit her. But it was the sickness that drove her to run—the crawling, the panic, the bugs under her skin. The sickness came when Grace didn't. And Grace didn't come because Wendy questioned God.

But God could have stopped it.

If He was God.

Not Mr. Dream, not Noah…

Mr. Dream snagged in Wendy's mind like a hangnail

catching a sleeve, pulling, threatening to rip flesh. Mister like a man you could spit at. Dream like a joke.

Wendy swallowed again and forced the thought down.

God was God.

She didn't drink.

Not yet.

Blasphemy and sin must be burned away. So, let the dryness burn. Let it be penance. Relief had to be earned.

Horn had said there was a room.

A ritual.

An end.

The tunnel didn't feel that big. But it kept going. Her lantern flickered. Fading. Refueled a few times. Her hand, slick with soot as the lantern belched the deep smoke.

Cassie's singing continued, soft and persistent, like the cave walls remembered her better than Wendy had a right to.

Wendy's eyelids grew heavy. The lullaby slid under her ribs, warm and wrong. She found herself humming along—raspy, thin, matching Cassie's angel voice with her own ruined one.

Then the tunnel widened.

Not much at first—just enough for Wendy's hips to fit

without wiggling through. Then her shoulders stopped scraping against the walls. Finally, she stood upright, stepping out of the cramped coffin opening into something that felt like a hallway.

And there, in the lantern's glow, Wendy saw the first sign she wasn't alone.

A body sat slumped against the wall.

Jumpsuit. Once white. Now ripped to threads. Gashes up the legs, tears across the arms. Mud crusted the fabric. The man's flesh was still there, but it had gone tough and leathery, peeled in strips like something had worried at it.

Wendy pressed her hearing into the tunnel beyond. No scurrying. No wings. No breathing besides her own.

If an animal had clawed his face and arms, why hadn't it eaten the rest?

Wendy's head followed the angle of the dead body's head until her neck cracked. She rubbed the base of her skull where the pop still radiated pain.

Then she saw the dark gash cut across the body's throat.

The same ornate knife Wendy carried rested in his hand, fingers stiff around the hilt like he'd held on through the end.

Wendy crouched and shifted the lantern closer.

No tremor in her hands. No sudden nausea. Only the quakes and aches of dope sickness creeping in. Seeing death wasn't new. The Sleep House had made corpses ordinary. People died and stayed where they fell until someone pitched the body outside, or down to the Basement Dwellers.

The name sent shivers through her.

Basement Dwellers.

They lurked in darkness like this.

Again, she listened.

Again, she heard nothing.

Wendy checked the satchel at the body's hip.

In the Sleep House, you didn't wait for someone to be cold before you searched them. Here, at least, there was no one to fight for the man's things.

His satchel was empty save for the journal and broken pen. Both exactly like the ones in her satchel.

Her hand reached for the notebook before she could stop it. Worn cover. Soft with use. Every page filled.

Those were his thoughts. Perhaps his last thoughts. Never meant for her.

What could he have known? The growth coiled within. *He found the way out. He found the room. Here's the map.*

Wendy's fingers tightened, then released. She tossed the notebook down beside the slumped body. Stood. Stepped past him and continued into the darkness.

Questions didn't form in her mind. Not about what had shredded his face. Not about whether he'd done it to himself. Not about why the knife sat in his hand like an answer.

All she took from the body was the message it left in the hallway:

Something dangerous lived in the tunnel.

Wendy slid her own knife free, gripped it hard enough to make her knuckles ache, and kept walking.

TWELVE

Hours passed with no branches. No choices. Just the same tunnel dragging her forward, turning and narrowing, then widening, then narrowing again like the cave was breathing around her.

Her lantern threw light against the mica in the walls, and the flecks answered back—cold, glittering. Stars that weren't stars. They blinked as she moved, watching her descent.

How deep could this cave even be?

Horn gave her supplies for a few days—as if the cave could eat time that easily. As if getting lost was the only reason she'd be down here long enough to need all of it. But how could she get lost? There was only one way to go.

That should have been comforting. It wasn't.

Wendy walked, one boot in front of the other, the lantern's handle biting into her palm.

Cassie once told her about a sweat lodge in Arizona. She described it as a place designed to crack into other dimensions, let other worlds bleed through. Cassie had described it like it was magic. Like stepping into a cave full of stars.

"Did you ever have a vision?" Wendy asked her.

Cassie nodded eagerly. "It told me to come here," she said. Her eyes were fixed on the basement.

"They won't hurt you," Wendy lied. She didn't see any of the Basement Dwellers lurking in the shadows, but they could have been just out of sight.

"I know," Cassie whispered. "You're my Guardian Angel."

Some fucking angel.

They started low—one roll of nerves sliding down her spine—then spread into her limbs. By the time the tremor reached her toes, another wave had already begun at her shoulders. Each surge chased the last, slow and drowning, until her whole body felt flooded with crawling electricity.

"How far?" she asked the cave.

It didn't answer.

Rain.

She realized she hadn't heard it in a long time.

At first the patter had followed her down here. Constant. Comforting in its own way, proof the outside still existed. Somewhere along the descent it had faded so gradually she hadn't noticed. Now the silence where it should've been made her skin tighten.

Wendy turned her head back.

Beyond the lantern's reach was nothing—pure black, swallowing the tunnel behind her. Farther off, points of light flickered, echoing the lantern's flame…or pretending to. Mica catching firelight, pretending to be stars. The cave lying about distance, about direction, about escape.

This wasn't Ascension.

It was descent.

She was walking slowly into a pit.

But she'd been lower before. The Sleep House taught her what dark, deep, cold felt like. The basement door. The threshold. That first memory—coming up from below and finding the foyer full of bodies and mold and worship—coiled her spine with the old terror of being seen.

The Basement Dwellers watched her ascend from the basement…Wendy shoved the thought away.

At least down here she could walk. At least there was only one way. No branches. Just the path.

She found a rock that rose out of the tunnel floor like a seat and lowered herself onto it, chest heaving. The lantern flame held steady, small and stubborn.

Pills.

Horn's rule: when the shakes start, take two. Only two.

Wendy dug the orange bottle out of her satchel with fingers that didn't want to work. She tapped out two pills into her palm.

She counted what remained.

Six.

A cold drop slid through her belly.

When had she last taken them? How long had she been walking? How many doses did "a few days" become in a place that ate hours?

She swallowed the pills dry, then forced herself to sip water. The water landed like a stone in her stomach. She took a long pull of protein drink—chalk thick, coating her tongue—and stood again.

The pills worked fast, smoothing the shakes down to a hum she could ignore.

Wendy kept walking.

Like the Sleep House, time lost meaning here.

The lantern's flame didn't change, but Wendy's sense of it did. Minutes stretched. Hours snapped. Her body moved and moved and moved until she couldn't tell if she'd been down here for half a day or half a week.

"I am on the Path of Ascension," she said to the dark. "I'm on the Path...the right path?"

The cave didn't answer.

It only kept swallowing.

The next body was fresher.

A woman.

Her jumpsuit was cleaner than Wendy's, cleaner even than the first corpse Wendy had passed—as if she hadn't crawled through the tunnel long enough to get fully claimed by it. Flesh hung in dry strands from bone. Her face had sunk in on itself, mouth open.

What was she saying when she died?

Wendy crouched and searched the satchel.

A piece of bread lay inside—stale, spotted with mold, but still bread. Wendy's stomach turned at the thought of eating it…

You will need that, the growth in her said. It coiled, warmed. She agreed with it. She tucked the bread away.

A pill bottle rattled in the bottom of the satchel.

Empty.

Wendy stared at the empty bottle longer than she meant to.

What skin remained around the woman's wrists was shredded and dark. The same kind of ruin Wendy had seen on the first body. Not animal teeth. Not claws. Something deliberate. The kind of damage a person did when pain made their mind small and desperate.

The clawing, digging, shredding Cassie did to her arms to let the bugs out.

Without the pills, Horn had said, the sickness always came back—and worse. Because Grace wasn't Heroin. It wasn't Crack. It was something darker, made from darker things in darker places.

And it didn't break as easily.

Dope-sick was deadly.

The shakes. The vomit. Confusion. Muscles clenching like they wanted to tear themselves out of your skin.

Wendy's mouth went dry.

There was no surviving the sickness. Not if it was patient. Not if it waited you out.

Wendy pried the woman's knife from her limp hand. She stared at the crimson crust lining the blade. It spiraled where the woman's blood drooled over it.

The second body. The second blood crusted knife. Wendy ran her fingers over her knife, still clean, still unused.

For now.

She didn't stay long enough to let the thought grow teeth.

The shakes quivered through Wendy's fingertips again—

little warning sparks—but she ignored them. She held her knife, gripping until her palm ached. The ache gave her something real to focus on.

Take pills only when you can't keep moving.

That was the rule now. Four pills left.

Wasn't it six?

Did she lose two? Did she take them and forget? Time slipped. The doses slipped with it. She searched for the memory of those pills.

But only found Cassie's voice.

"Have you ever tried to leave here?" Cassie asked once in the library—before the stairs, before the sin, when questions were safe.

"Anyone can leave anytime," Wendy repeated, parroting the lie everyone recited. You could leave. You just couldn't come back.

And where would you go?

Wendy had taken a long drag from a cigarette dipped in Grace and handed it to Cassie. Cassie smoked and her pupils bloomed, shrinking the amber brown in her eyes to a thin outline. This wasn't just from the drug, but from suddenly understanding how insane the question was.

Why leave the only place that gave you dreamless nothing?

God asked for worship. That was all. Kneel when He came down. Keep your head low. Don't cross Him. The rules weren't many, but they were sharp.

Wendy's mind drifted through the Sleep House the way it used to drift through rooms: library where you could pretend to be wise; kitchen where the workers hauled trash cans of food and filled the gray bowls; foyer where the lost lay waiting; under the stairs where sinners were shoved out of sight; basement where the ones beyond Grace survived on darkness and whatever the nothing down there chose to give back.

Cassie had leaned closer, whispering like conspirators. "Why did you come here?"

"I don't know," Wendy said, and the truth slipped out so easily it scared her.

Cassie sighed, contented but curious. "Come on. You can tell me. I won't judge—"

"No," Wendy snapped. She took the cigarette, letting the numbness smother the conversation. "I just was here."

"Where were you before?"

Wendy shrugged, careless because Grace made everything careless. "Probably nowhere good."

But her mind had drifted down and down, toward the basement, toward the white glare before that—fire—voices—

Wendy shoved the memory shut and found herself standing

in the tunnel again, lantern in hand, knives in her bag, bodies behind her like mile markers.

These were people from the Sleep House.

They'd failed Ascension.

Why?

Had they run out of pills? Had they panicked? Had the tunnel turned them around until they couldn't tell up from down? Had their faith finally snapped and left them empty?

Would Ascension reward her?

Wendy tried to hold the idea of reward and felt it slide around inside her like something slick.

God.

She reached for God the way she'd always reached.

And found Yacob instead.

Olive skin. Curly black hair. His knee on the floor beside hers. Hands folded wrong like hers. His voice kind in the way that made Wendy's throat ache.

"God's always listening," he'd told her. "But He's watching everyone. Sometimes you gotta pick yourself up and keep going while God's helping someone who needs Him more."

Wendy's steps slowed.

When had the God of the Sleep House helped anyone?

He didn't.

He punished. He stomped a man to death beside Wendy's bowed head. He fed people poison and watched them drown in their own vomit. He smiled while doing it.

Was Yacob wrong?

Or had Wendy been worshipping something that was never God at all?

Noah.

The thought split open inside her.

Her throat trembled—not from sickness this time, but from tears rising too fast.

A sob tore out of her.

Hot. Loud. Embarrassing.

She bent forward, shoulders shaking, lantern light wobbling on the walls as tears spilled down her cheeks.

When had she last cried? Grace had kept her numb for so long she'd forgotten what it felt like to break. But the mountain's clarity—the cave's clarity—dragged everything back: memory, feeling, regret.

The loss of herself was a weight pressing her ribs inward. Years wasted. Fear wasted. Worship wasted.

Betrayal poured in behind it.

The Bionic Woman lunchbox flashed in her mind—the baggies she'd hidden, the Grace she'd hoarded. What she'd kept to herself when it could've saved someone else.

It would have saved Cassie.

Wendy staggered forward, letting the sobs echo down the tunnel.

The sound came back hollow and alone.

And still, she kept walking.

THIRTEEN

Her feet were wet.

Not water. There was no water in the cave, but her socks were soaked. The heat trapped in her socks and boots cooked the dampness until it was slick, wrong.

Every step was walking on glass. Broken shards shifting in her boots, in her socks, in her skin.

Something dug in.

Glass. Stone. Bone. It didn't matter. The pain was the same: a corroded, rusty nail lancing up her legs, making her vision pulse.

Wendy's knees buckled.

She slammed against the tunnel floor. The impact punched the breath from her chest, leaving a burning emptiness. Vertigo flooded through her, filling the spaces air could not fit.

Lantern light jumped across mica flecks—cold stars blinking at her collapse.

How long since the last dead body?

Hours? Days? Weeks?

Time—the thought slid away before she could finish it.

She yanked off her boot.

No water leaked out. No bright shard clinked out. Just the stink of old sweat, dirt—then it came. The foul, sickly-sweet reek. It filled her nose. Coated her throat. Too close to the fruit Mr. Dream salvaged from dumpsters. The food he'd dump in the foyer at feeding time.

But the smell made her stomach remember food. It clenched. Hungry. Empty. Seizing from the sickness building within her.

Yes, eat it, the growth said. *Eat the rot.*

She peeled her sock over her heel.

A wet sucking sound followed.

Not fabric on skin—fabric on drooling meat.

The sock clung to the thick wetness.

Wendy hissed through her teeth and ripped the sock away.

Pain flared white-hot. Her foot jerked.

The sock came off. Tearing. Popping. Popping pouring more sickly-sweet rotten fruit stink into the air.

Blisters—fat, swollen bubbles—erupted across her heel and the ball of her foot. The sock had fused to them. Ripping the sock away peeled her feet like the skin of a bruised apple.

Yellowed liquid wept out first, thick and warm, then

thinner—mixed with blood where the raw flesh tore. The smell twisted her guts. She no longer thought of eating dumpster fruit.

Wendy stared at her foot as if it belonged to someone else.

Then the pain caught up. She screamed at the ruined flesh, the hunger still lingering within her, the razors in her feet.

If only she could be numb again. Feel the nothing Grace brought. If only she had…

Just a taste…

Burning pain throbbed in waves, each pulse making her toes curl.

The other boot.

The other sock.

Just a taste, the growth said. *You can find it in here. Just look.*

"No," Wendy whimpered. Self-loathing crushed her soul.

She wanted it. She needed it. Not just a taste. She needed Grace to coat her gums. To let the numbness bloom over her and to sleep the dreamless sleep.

The mountain freed her. And now she wanted to go back. Back to sleep. Back to the rot. Back to death.

"No!"

Wendy slammed her foot on the stone ground. Pain roared through her, twisting her stomach. Penance for weakness. For wanting to be who she was and throw away the freedom Horn's given her. The mountain has given her.

The stone's cool should have soothed her.

It didn't.

And she relished the torment.

Wendy slid off the rock she sat on. She slumped on the floor.

Like the dead bodies.

Her satchel lay where it had fallen, straps twisted like a snapped limb.

Like the dead bodies.

She could reach her knife. The final thing needed to make her into just another dead body. Faithless. Failures in Ascension.

Every tendon in her legs vibrated. The muscles in her back burned. Her shoulders strained to keep from hunching. Her throat was dry from rationing water. Her stomach empty from doing the same with her protein shake. Sleep was a distant memory having pushed herself forward, knowing ascension was just around the next curve.

Except it wasn't.

It never was.

Horn said it was there. God said it was there. The mountain said nothing.

Wendy swallowed hard and thought of Cassie. Of Yacob. Of the fact that she'd forgotten a man who'd called her Firecracker like it was praise and not a warning.

Was he alive? Was he looking? Would he even recognize her now?

What did happen to her?

The sickness answered.

Every muscle in her body wrenched tight, curling her into a ball. She fell over. A hot cramp seized her gut and twisted until sparks flared behind her clenched eyelids.

The shakes unraveled in her like writhing snakes springing from a trap.

She couldn't hold it back anymore.

The pills had to last—

—but she'd waited too long.

Wendy clawed at her satchel, yanked it close, tore it open, found the orange bottle by feel. Childproof lid. Her hands were a storm. Fingers missing their targets.

She twisted.

Nothing.

She twisted harder. Straining. Groaning with the effort.

The lid snapped wrong.

Plastic cracking.

Top popped off.

Pills skittered across stone like teeth.

"No!" Wendy gasped.

They bounced and rolled into crevices, under her knee, out of the lantern's small circle of light. She dove after them on her ruined feet, the raw skin sliding over rock. Pain sliced through her.

The world shrank to a pin hole of light, circling two pills near her hand.

She went for them.

Missed.

Another shockwave wracked her. Her fingers spasmed open and shut. They weren't hers. They belonged to the sickness.

It didn't want the pills. It wanted her to suffer.

The growth within laughed. Wet. Gurgling. Dripping with joy.

Wendy grunted, forcing the sound out of her throat. She was in control. Not the sickness.

She was in control.

Say it again.

She was in control.

She tried again—fingers trembling, but obeying, she pinched one pill and jammed it into her mouth.

It stuck to her tongue.

Dry as chalk.

Her throat refused it.

She gagged, heaved, and the pill caught on the barbs in her throat. It wouldn't drop.

Wendy growled and forced it down with sheer will until it finally slid—slow and painful—into her stomach.

Another pill lay near her palm.

She snatched it and swallowed just as roughly.

Water.

She needed water or she'd vomit them back up.

The satchel was too far, and her feet—

No. Don't think about feet. Move.

Wendy scurried on her hands and knees. The sickness surged behind her eyes, making the lantern flame blur.

She found a bottle. Unscrewed it. Drank.

Cold water hit her throat. Clean. Fresh. She gulped like an animal.

Too fast.

Her stomach convulsed.

Vomit rose hot and sudden into her mouth.

Wendy swallowed it down.

The pills can't be lost.

She drank again, drowning the bile with cold water and stubbornness.

Her gut fought harder, rolling the pills against her teeth with acid and panic. She tilted her head back toward the ceiling, grit her few remaining teeth, and swallowed hard—again and again—until she felt the pills drop into her stomach with a hollow, ugly thud.

She roared, and the echo ran down the tunnel and came back thinner, twisted into a hideous laugh.

The cave was laughing.

The mountain, laughing.

She tried to roar again.

It became a scream.

Pleading.

Then her body won.

Wendy vomited.

There wasn't much—protein drink, water, stomach acid. It splashed onto the stone in a pale brown, goopy puddle that steamed faintly in the lantern's heat.

Wendy whimpered.

Not because of the puke—because she'd failed something simple: *keep it down.*

The pills.

Her eyes locked on the puddle.

She crawled to it and plunged her fingers into the warm sludge, gagging as the stink met her nose. She fished through the goop until she felt hard chalk.

A pill.

Another.

Slick with vomit and grit.

Her hands shook harder. Her nails scraped stone. She pinched the pills.

They crumbled.

Soft and useless in her fingers.

"Fuck," Wendy whispered.

She shoved the crumbled mess into her mouth, chasing it with water, swallowing dirt and bile and chalk because the alternative was the knife.

Where were the other pills?

Not in the puddle.

Not on the floor.

Gone.

Her whole body trembled as the sickness didn't let go.

Before, the pills had snapped her back into steadiness. This time the sickness clung to her. Even the pills couldn't pry its bite from her throat.

It wanted her to stop moving.

The growth laughed harder. It pressed hard against her ribs, digging to find the way out.

It wanted her to lie down like the others.

The laughter echoed around her. Louder and louder until heat split through her chest. The growth uncoiling, lashing through her bones in a splintering cackle. Its laughter filled the cave around her now. Echoing from the walls.

The knife was in the satchel.

She could end it. Quick. Clean. Quiet.

This is how they ended.

The laughter died. The echo thinned into silence.

Then a man's voice said, close and calm: "Be careful making so much noise."

Wendy froze. Every muscle locked.

Was that in her head?

Or ahead?

Or behind?

She'd crawled. Spun. Vomited. Scrambled. The tunnel had turned itself into a loop in her mind.

Which way was out?

Which way was deeper?

Her footprints—smears of mud and blood and pus—were everywhere.

"Who's there?" Wendy demanded, her voice cracking.

"A fellow lost soul like you," the man said.

Confident voice. The kind that enjoyed being heard. The kind that didn't waste time taking what it wanted once it decided it wanted you.

"I'm not lost," Wendy said.

She grabbed her knife, fingers slick, grip tight.

"You look lost," the voice replied. "Wandering down here. That isn't safe."

Wendy held the blade up. Could he even see it? Where was he? "If you don't buzz off, you won't be safe either."

A hearty chuckle answered—unbothered, unthreatened.

Could he see her shaking?

Her feet flayed open?

She couldn't stand, much less fight—

—but she would try.

Wendy pushed herself upright, climbing the wall behind her.

Her feet screamed as raw flesh met stone. A fresh rupture split somewhere on her heel and hot wet pain shot up her calf. She grabbed the wall, nails scraping rock, holding herself up.

A shadow slithered through the lantern glow.

Snake?

Wendy kicked instinctively—

Her foot hit the lantern.

Glass shattered.

Flame died.

Darkness swallowed the tunnel.

His chuckling grew, bouncing off stone, suffocating Wendy. Impossible to place.

Wendy lashed out, swinging blindly.

Her knife struck the wall—sparked bright orange for a blink—and in that blink she saw teeth.

Drool-coated. Smiling.

Death's grin.

Then dark again.

"Come on!" Wendy screamed. "I'm not dying here! So come get this in your guts!"

"No need," the man sighed. "Come. Let us talk of these matters in a civilized manner. No guts must be spilled, yes?"

The last word rose into a high-pitched giggle.

Familiar.

Too familiar.

Wendy clenched her chest.

A pale blue glow pulsed ahead—dimmer than the beacons on the mountain, sickly, ghost-colored. Not sanctuary. Only *direction.*

Horn had said: go to the light.

"Come to us," the voice said. "We have a meal prepared."

Behind her: dark.

Ahead: ghost blue.

And Horn's men outside the cave mouth—guns, probably. Rules. The Order. No leaving until the ritual was done.

Wendy raised the knife and lurched forward.

She struck the wall again—spark—and checked behind her.

No one.

The tunnel curved gently, leading her like a hand on the back of her neck. She followed it, dragging her ruined feet through grit. Every step was glass. Every pebble a needle in raw meat. Pus made her soles slip. Blood made the rock tacky.

Wendy kept moving.

Then she saw the source of the light.

A long dinner table.

Set in the tunnel like a joke.

Her knife fell, clattering on the floor.

Faces turned toward her—mostly familiar, faces. Two faces she didn't recognize – but the haze of memory cleared enough for her to know one.

Everyone smiled at Wendy.

Except one.

One of the smiling faces was a man Wendy didn't recognize. He stood at the end of the table, grinning.

"Wendy," he said warmly, expecting her. Like she was late. "So glad you could join us."

It was the voice from the darkness.

"Please," he said, gesturing toward the chair at the end of the long rectangular table. "Please. Have a seat."

The chair was open.

Waiting.

Meant for her.

The guest of honor.

FOURTEEN

Wendy didn't move.

Her knife lay somewhere behind her in the tunnel. Her lantern was dead. Her feet throbbed in wet pulses, each heartbeat ringing through the raw skin like a bell.

And the table waited.

What the hell was this?

Real?

The room was too clean for the cave. A wide cavern tiled blue up to the waist, white above, as if someone had tried to turn stone into a bathroom. A chandelier hung over the center—real candles, pale flames, soft and patient. Their light didn't flicker like fire should in a cave. There was no wind. No breeze. Only still air.

In the middle sat a long dark-wood dinner table. Big enough for ten.

Only five sat there.

Her mother.

Yacob.

Cassie.

Mr. Dream—God without his light, without his halo, just a man in a nice suit. Noah.

And the Stranger.

They sat in ornate wooden chairs with red velvet cushions. Each place setting held a silver platter covered by a silver dome. No forks. No knives. No napkins. No salt. No pepper. Only polished domes, smooth and bright.

The Stranger watched Wendy as if she were late to something important.

He wore a red silk shirt and black slacks, top button open, chest hair dark against pale skin. His curls were tight and neat. His eyes were gray—storm-water—and his smile was easy in the way dealers smiled when your lips quivered before the price was mentioned.

Everyone but her mother smiled at Wendy, inviting.

Her mother didn't look up.

Cassie motioned to the chair at the head of the table. "Come on, Wendy. Sit with us."

"Yeah, Firecracker," Yacob said softly. His voice was exactly where Wendy had left it in her memory—warm, stubborn, kind. "Come have something to eat. You look like you could use a real meal."

Mr. Dream nodded like a gentleman agreeing with good manners. Without his light, his divinity looked like costume jewelry. A suit. A smile. Hands folded neatly, like he'd never stomped anyone to death. As if he wouldn't make you kill your only friend. Or force you to keep living after you did.

The Stranger leaned forward. "Yes," he said. "Sit, Wendy. This is your Ascension Feast." His tone made Feast sound like a contract. "And you wouldn't want to keep your guests waiting, would you?"

Wendy's stomach clenched.

Food.

Real food.

The smell leaked from under the domes—savory, heavy, wet with promise. Her mouth flooded. Her tongue ached. Her knees softened. Her body dipped toward the chair before she decided to sit. Bleeding feet were ready to rest.

Chicken?

Roast beef?

Turkey.

Yacob had made Thanksgiving dinner once. He'd let Wendy help. He'd handed her a spoon and treated her like she mattered, that she wouldn't just screw it up. That she wasn't just another problem in a life full of problems.

How could she not remember that day? It was the perfect day. But only now had the mists of memory cleared, revealing Yacob.

Wendy stared at the domes and wanted to believe this was that day.

Wanted it so badly her heart strained to make it so.

But there were no side dishes. No bowls. No utensils. No gravy. Nothing ordinary.

Just domes.

Just waiting.

This wasn't real.

Her feet throbbed. Her legs shook from holding herself upright. Her stomach squeezed with hunger and sickness. The chair was salvation for her broken body.

And somewhere behind her there was an exit—dark and ugly and honest.

Wendy turned her head toward the tunnel.

It couldn't be far.

She could limp.

She could drag herself back the way she'd come.

She could crawl.

She could leave.

The thought bloomed bright for one second—

—and then her mind pictured it: the tunnel forever, the pills running out, the bodies, the knife, the cave swallowing her. Leaving didn't mean freedom. Leaving meant dying alone where no one would even find her.

Wendy's throat tightened.

She should go.

But she couldn't.

Not if this was the trial. Not if walking away meant failing. Meant becoming just another corpse on the Path to Ascension.

"If you must go, you must," Yacob said.

The words landed on Wendy heavy, sorrowful.

The same sorrow Wendy remembered from the last time she'd heard him say it.

She was a kid again for a heartbeat.

Her mother screaming outside the door. A new boyfriend in the driveway. Threats about the police. Accusations thrown at Yacob like knives—kidnapper, pervert, sick—none of it true, all of it loud enough to make the scene her mother always wanted.

Wendy had gotten into her mother's car before Yacob could answer because fear made choices for you.

Yacob had reached out, not grabbing her, not forcing her— just trying to hold her in the world a second longer.

If you must go, you must.

Wendy's chest tightened like it did back then.

She looked at the tunnel again.

Then she turned back.

She sat.

Her chair accepted her with a soft embrace on her back and bottom. All her weight was taken from her feet, from her body. Relief poured through her. A sound slipped out of her—small, grateful, ashamed.

Yacob smiled at her and reached out a hand.

Wendy took it.

His touch was cool and unreal—mist against skin—yet it filled her anyway, a warmth that didn't belong in a cave. Love without a price tag.

Cassie reached for Wendy too, sitting to her right.

Wendy took Cassie's hand.

Cassie's was solid. Warm. Real enough to hurt.

Wendy's throat worked. "I'm—"

Cassie squeezed her fingers like she didn't need words.

The Stranger clapped once, delighted. "And so," he said. "Let the feast commence."

FIFTEEN

After the Stranger's clap, silver domes lifted in unison.

The sound was small—polished metal sliding off polished metal— but Wendy's body seized—breath knocked out of her, every muscle locking. Her stomach surged. Bile flooded her mouth, hot and bitter. She swallowed, fighting the strain in her throat to shove her disgust back down.

Then the smell hit.

Not one smell. A pile of them. Sweet and rotten. Copper and sour milk. Antiseptic and meat. It rolled across the table in a humid wave, turning the air into something you had to chew to breathe.

And then Wendy's eyes caught the movement. Every platter was alive, except one. She couldn't look at that one. Her mind tried shut down. To escape into the darkness, to the numbness, but she only found this room, the tunnel's end and could not escape.

Her mother's platter held a struggling baby.

Not clean. Not wrapped. Skin slick with chunky birth-jelly, mottled with purple and pink as if it hadn't decided what color it belonged to yet. The umbilical cord still attached—long and drooling gore—writhing in lazy serpentine lashes as if it had muscles of its own. The smell was sweet and metallic and wrong, like pennies dropped into spoiled fruit.

Her mother sighed like she'd been served the wrong entree. Disappointed. Annoyed. She gathered the cord in her hand and wrapped it around her wrist with practiced impatience, the end vanishing into her skin as if her wrists had always been open there.

Yacob's platter held a beating heart.

A real one—bloody and blackened and too alive. It seized around a steak knife buried through its center, the blade pinning it like a specimen. Every pulse jerked the whole thing hard enough to rattle the silver platter. Yacob braced the knife with both hands, jaw tight, arms straining to hold it on his plate. Each beat sounded like a fist hammering squelching meat.

Thump. Thump. Thump.

Wendy's throat tightened. Her feet throbbed under the table, matching the heartbeat. She tried to stand, but her feet screamed when they touched the cold floor and her legs did nothing but quiver.

Mr. Dream's platter was ashy flesh.

Not meat—living skin.

A hemorrhaging blister rose out of it, black around the

edges, swollen and obscene. Yellow pus seeped from a split seam and slid in slow ropes down the curve, pooling at the base like a lazy promise. The stink was chemical and infected—old needles, old rot, the sharp tang of medicine gone bad.

Mr. Dream didn't flinch.

He picked up his single utensil—a syringe—and held it the way a man holds a fork when he's eager.

Cassie's dome lifted.

Wendy's eyes refused. She couldn't look. It had to be the worst. It had to be the manifestation of betrayal, of murder, of cowardice. Wendy whimpered. She kept her eyes on Cassie's, searching for relief, or absolution, or something to escape seeing her meal.

Cassie smiled down at it with that crooked grin Wendy had missed so hard the sight of it surged tears in her eyes, in her throat.

Wendy couldn't inhale.

Her hand pressed to where the growth always coiled, where it burned. The place under her ribs was quiet. Empty.

She turned her stare to the Stranger. Her mind couldn't break if she focused on him. Her soul wouldn't slip away facing him and playing his games. Just another dealer trying to fuck her.

Nothing more.

The Stranger's platter held two objects laid neatly beside each other: a needle and a key.

The needle was empty. Clean. Waiting.

The key was small and rusted and ordinary—simple teeth, spiral handle—like it belonged to a cheap padlock on a cheap door. The kind of key you lose until it matters.

Wendy's plate sat in front of her, untouched.

She didn't look at it. Didn't need to look.

She knew the heat crawling up from it, the faint shimmer of something that wanted to be inside her.

The Stranger folded his hands as if they were at a normal dinner. "Each of them will eat until they are full," he said, voice pleasant. "They will feast."

His gaze slid to Wendy, and Wendy felt it like a hand at the base of her skull.

"When you want them to stop, you tell me." He tapped the empty needle with one finger. "When you are ready to finish, you may have yours and be done."

The Stranger motioned to her plate, and Wendy dropped her eyes. It was what she thought. Smelling of burnt plastic chemicals and darkness and numbness. Her plate was a boiling mass of Grace.

The Stranger lifted the key, tapping it on his platter. She

looked. He said, "But if you make it through all the courses…" His smile widened just a fraction. "You can leave."

Behind him, a door appeared.

Not magical—worse. Plain. Frail wood slats tied together with frayed rope. The kind of door that shouldn't exist in a cave, the kind of door you could kick apart if you were strong enough.

Wendy stared at it until her eyes burned.

"And if I want to leave now?" she asked. Her voice was weak, desperate for what was right in front of her. The Grace's scent, a toxic sweetness slid down her throat reminding her of better times under the stairs when she faced nothing but her own vomit and Death. The pills had softened the sickness, but it still lived inside her, waiting. Wanting.

"You can." The Stranger raised the empty needle, pointing toward her platter. "Any time."

Mr. Dream examined the tip of his syringe closely, smiling approval.

Her mother tightened her fist around the cord.

Yacob held the knife like it anchored him to earth.

Cassie's hand hovered over her plate, eager, trusting, wrong.

Wendy pulled in a slow breath through her nose and tasted it all again—the rot-sweet, the copper, the infection, the warm meat air—and she understood, in the deepest place she understood:

This wasn't dinner.

This was how they were going to break her.

She settled back into the chair, forced her shaking hands flat on the table, and kept her eyes on the Stranger.

Wendy nodded.

"Then let's begin," the Stranger said.

SIXTEEN

The baby cried.

Not a normal cry—a needle-scream that went straight through Wendy's skull, scraping the inside of her eyes. The sound bounced off tile and stone and candlelight and came back sharper. The room amplified the shrieks. Each wail made Wendy's already-raw throat tighten and her blistered feet throb in sympathy under the table, pain pulsing in wet rings.

Nobody else flinched.

They looked at the baby with the passing interest of a late dish. Something sent back and when it returned, it was still wrong.

Her mother's hand spasmed where the umbilical cord vanished into her wrist.

"I didn't expect a good child," her mother said, old exhaustion crushing her voice. "No kids are." She jerked her chin at the baby. "But you screamed and screamed and hated me so much you never let me sleep. No one would take you because you screamed nonstop. I lost my job because you couldn't let me go."

Lump after lump slowly wriggled up the cord—dragging nourishment out of her mother's wrist. The baby's mouth worked soundlessly between screams, sucking and sucking like it could drink the world dry.

With every swallow, the baby screamed harder.

Wendy's stomach rolled. Bile climbed her tongue, bitter and hot. The smell rising off that platter wasn't food. It was birth and blood and something sweet-sour—milk gone wrong. Copper. Wet skin. The kind of stink that lives under bandages.

Her mother kept talking, louder now, trying to be heard over the wail. The tone was exactly as Wendy remembered it: strained, worn thin, angry with no place to put the anger but at her.

Wendy watched the truth happen in front of her.

The cord's bulges grew bigger. Faster. Her mother's wrist darkened to bruised black, then gray. The skin on her hand went slack. Loose. Sagging. It didn't fit anymore. Blonde curls thinned into stringy white wisps. Her cheeks hollowed as if an invisible hand were scooping her out from the inside.

Not a vampire.

A vampire would finish the job.

This thing didn't kill quickly. It fed slow.

"You made me need to escape," her mother said, and her voice cracked—not with emotion, with dehydration. "And when I couldn't leave because they kept bringing you back to me, I left in my mind." She tried to cry, but there were no tears left.

The cord pulsed again. Her mother's forearm caved, collapsing in on itself.

"You didn't stop," she went on. "You got older and you still needed me. All the time. I couldn't take it." Her lips pulled tight over her teeth. "So, I found things that made me lighter. Made you smaller. I drank them, smoked them, shot them—anything to get away. And then—" her eyes unfocused, drifting into a private joy "—the last pop finally let me get away forever."

She sighed.

Content.

That fucking sigh grated against Wendy's mind. Her mother could have cussed her out, could have spit on her, and it wouldn't have been as insulting, as obscene as that sigh.

Her mother's skin turned papery. Dust flaked off her knuckles. She slumped forward, shoulder collapsing like wet cardboard. Her hand still held the cord, wrapped tight—ownership, habit, punishment—until the grip loosened and the cord slid through her fingers.

The baby screamed once more, ravenous, and then—

silence.

Her mother's head settled onto the tabletop like it was finally allowed to rest. A faint smile tugged her mouth—small, satisfied, relieved. Her lips split. No blood beaded or spilled, only skin flaked away.

Wendy saw the motel bathtub.

That same stillness. That same relief. That same smile that wasn't meant for Wendy.

Free.

Her mom smiled from the bathtub, eyes empty and white film dulling her once bright blues.

No goodbye. Just dead eyes. A dangling hand over the bathtub rim.

Leaving Wendy behind with strangers who traded children like currency, who took whatever they wanted because no one came to stop them.

Wendy's chest went tight. Her hands curled under the table until her nails bit her palms.

She drew a breath. It quaked through her body. The dusty cloud of her mother tasted sour-sweet, a ghost of her mother's smell in life filling her nose, loosening the words in her throat.

"You were weak," Wendy said.

Her voice surprised her—steady, low, not a scream.

"You cared more about getting away than what you left behind." Wendy's eyes stayed on the dusting shape of her mother. "You didn't love me. You loved not-feeling."

The words broke through her teeth as if waiting to erupt for years.

"You want to blame me for your choices? Fine." Wendy leaned forward. The candles didn't flicker. The room didn't breathe. "I was a baby. You were an adult. You made the deals. You brought the men. You picked the drugs. You picked leaving. I made peace with you being a shitty mother long ago."

A flash hit Wendy—salt air, sunlight, the ocean. Her mother laughing. An arcade. Sticky fingers. Ice cream melting down Wendy's wrist. Her mother buying another without making Wendy earn it. A man chasing them playfully across sand— smiling too. Wendy knew he was her dad and still couldn't see his face.

The memory hurt in a way the cave hadn't struck her before. The cave tore her feet apart. It exhausted her body. But now it dug at her mind, her memory of the horrible mother who got her ice cream and smiled once and laughed once. And a father. More than just some dealer. A man her mom loved. A family that was happy.

Her…family?

"So selfish of me," her mother's voice said, thin as ash. "I spent our rent on a trip to the ocean for you." A faint, brittle laugh. "Yet you remember I wasn't all bad."

Then her mouth crumbled.

Her cheek collapsed.

Her head broke into powder and scattered like the room had exhaled.

The baby was gone too.

No scream.

No cord.

No smell—only a lingering sour-sweet ghost in Wendy's nose.

Wendy sat frozen for a beat, staring at the empty chair where her mother had been.

There had been good moments.

A few.

They didn't cancel what came after.

What mother lets her daughter find her dead?

What mother hands her child to a man who'd rather sell her than keep her safe?

Wendy felt something loosen inside her—not forgiveness. Not grief.

Grief had been wrung out of her years ago.

What remained was a clean, hard hatred that didn't need to prove itself to anyone.

Wendy pulled in a sharp breath.

Some of the weight left her chest.

Most stayed.

She didn't look at her own plate.

Not yet.

She looked at the faces around the table.

The Stranger's fingers slid towards the needle.

But Wendy's gaze moved between the needle and the key.

The needle meant *stop*.

The key meant *through*.

Her blistered feet screamed under the table, and her body begged her to quit—but quitting was how she'd lived her whole life. Quitting was how her mother had made choices. Quitting was how Cassie had died.

Wendy pointed at the key.

The Stranger's smile deepened, pleased.

Wendy turned her eyes to Mr. Dream—Noah—God stripped down to a man with yellow teeth and a polite posture.

He smiled back.

And Wendy realized how much of him had been hidden behind light.

Wendy broke the silence.

"Next."

SEVENTEEN

Yacob grunted, both hands braced around the knife as if the blade were trying to escape.

"Need assistance?" the Stranger asked, voice pleasant.

Yacob shook his head. "I can do this."

"There's no shame in asking for help," Cassie said brightly.

The words slapped Wendy because she had said them to Cassie. And before that, Yacob said them to Wendy. They were the words he spoke to Wendy when she was small and scared and still believed adults didn't lie.

"No, dear," Yacob said gently. "Thank you."

He smiled—soft, tired—and pulled the knife free.

Blood arced out in a bright, sudden ribbon. Hot. Alive.

The heart on the platter gave one last violent jerk—then settled, motionless, like it had been waiting for permission to stop.

"I don't understand," Wendy said. Her voice came out thin and jagged. "Why are you here?"

Of everyone at the table, Yacob made the least sense.

She hadn't hurt him. Not with her hands. Not with her mouth. Not the way she'd hurt others.

He'd been a bright thing in the swamp of her life. A flower of goodness that hadn't asked her to bleed for it.

Yacob wasn't like her mother's other men. He'd been soft around the edges—chubby, balding, glasses, nice clothes that weren't showy. He gave money away instead of flashing it. Her mother used to complain about that, bitter and disgusted. *He gives too much to church. He wants me to stick around, he better be sending some of that cash my way.* She had hunted for a wealthy man and never understood that truly wealthy men didn't spend their worth on shiny proof.

Now Yacob's hands shook around the knife.

Not from weakness.

From what he was about to say.

"I didn't want to be here, Firecracker," he said.

His eyes flicked to the Stranger, then closed as if he couldn't bear looking at the shape of this room. "I shouldn't be here." He opened his eyes again and met Wendy's. "But you brought me."

Wendy's throat tightened.

"Never could say no to you," Yacob added, and tried to chuckle, but it came out empty.

"But you were good," Wendy whispered. Tears trembled at

her lashes. Her body quivered, more than dope-sick—eyelids, lips, fingers—betrayed her.

Yacob's voice stayed gentle. "Then why didn't you come back?"

The words landed clean.

No accusation. No punishment.

Just a question she'd been avoiding since she was twelve.

"I waited for you at the church," Yacob said. "I prayed your mom would come back—or at least you." His fist pressed to the tabletop to steady the shaking knife. "I waited."

On his platter, the heart didn't beat anymore.

But the knife in his hand did, almost—twitching, restless—it knew its purpose. It knew where it belonged.

Wendy tried to answer but her mouth shook too hard to form words. Her fingernails dug through her mind, attempting to discover an answer that wasn't the truth.

But as she clawed deeper, searching for anything else, she found nothing. All there was, was the horrible, horrible truth.

Her inescapable, certain truth.

"I…" Her breath scraped. "You wouldn't have wanted me."

Yacob's brows pulled together. "Why would you think that?"

Because men had touched her like she was an object and then tossed her away. Because she'd learned to keep rot inside her mouth, in her veins, and call it life. Because if Yacob looked at her, he'd see what she'd become and his kindness would curdle into disgust.

And the only good thing she'd ever known would be poisoned – just like everything else she touched.

"Mom left me," Wendy said. Her voice broke into shards. "With bad men. Evil men."

Mr. Dream—Noah—made a soft, pleased sound in his throat.

Wendy's head snapped toward him. Rage flashed hot. "Disgusting men," she spit, and the word tasted like bile. "Disgusting humans who made me—"

Her voice caught on a memory.

Rain.

Lightning.

A red door.

She was twelve again, feet blistered like now, body shaking from running miles on hunger and fear. She stood outside Yacob's church in a storm and stared at the lantern over the chapel door—a little beacon of warmth and safety.

She'd lifted her hand to knock.

And then she imagined it: the door opening, light spilling out, and someone seeing her. Smelling her. Asking where she'd been. What had happened.

They'd take her in. They'd call Yacob.

Yacob would look at her.

Yacob would know.

He'd retch, unable to stomach the foul gremlin who stole his sweet Wendy's body, her mind, her soul.

She couldn't bear that moment. When his love turned to revulsion. She couldn't bear infecting him with her filth.

So, she lowered her hand.

Stepped back from the light.

And walked into the rain until the cold stopped feeling like anything.

She returned to the darkness because darkness didn't ask questions.

At the table, Wendy's hands clenched so hard her nails bit her palms. Blood drooled, thick and lazy, between her fingers.

Wendy said hoarsely, "I didn't come back because I didn't want to ruin you."

Yacob's face changed—pain, yes, but not disgust. Never disgust.

His voice softened further, impossibly. "Firecracker…"

Tears spilled down Wendy's face at the name, the softness.

"I love your spark. Your fiery mind. Your curiosity. Your brilliance. I love you. And that could never be ruined," Yacob said.

The knife in his hand finally stopped trembling.

And Wendy realized the heart hadn't been the thing fighting.

It was the knife. It knew its purpose.

Yacob's hand slacked.

The knife, launched from the table, Yacob's hand still around it. The blade stabbed into his chest.

Wendy flinched, but no blood sprayed. His skin popped like a paper bag, dry and weak. Not a bag but a sigh as the knife split him. The wound opened into emptiness.

A void.

Cold air leaked out. Wendy understood what waiting did to him. It hollowed him out with years of unfulfilled expectations, of hope, and faith, and nothing.

"I waited for you," Yacob said, and his voice didn't break. "And I looked for you. I searched." He pushed the knife deeper, widening the hole, not with pain but with purpose. "But I couldn't find you."

"And so he built a way to find others," the Stranger said smoothly, as if this were a fun fact on a tour. "Wendy's Lost Girls. A nonprofit out of the church you used to attend. Still running."

Wendy tried to stand.

Her legs didn't listen.

She reached anyway, straining to get to him—her body pinned to the chair as if the cave would only permit her to watch.

"You did that?" Wendy choked. "For me?"

Yacob leaned across the table just enough that Wendy could brush his cheek with shaking fingers.

Her dirt crusted hand passed through his skin, damp mist trailing as her fingers worked to find him in the nothing.

"Salvation is for everyone," Yacob said quietly. "You don't get disqualified for being hurt." He set the knife down like it had never mattered. "I always knew you'd come back."

Wendy's throat made a small animal sound.

"Just thought it would've been before I died," Yacob added, and smiled—the same warm stubborn smile.

He kissed Wendy's hand.

Wendy grabbed for him. "No. Don't leave me again."

Yacob froze, and the sadness in his eyes was older than the cave, older than Ascension, as he spoke the most horrific truth yet. "Firecracker, I never left you." He tried to hold her hand, but his cold mist simply passed through her. "You just never came back to me."

He lifted the heart from the platter—heavy, wet, human—and tucked it into the void in his chest like returning a stolen thing to its rightful place.

"Remember what God taught us," he said.

Wendy's vision blurred. The hand from her dream flashed into her mind—reaching through dark, fingers straining for hers.

In the dream, it had been a woman's hand.

Not Yacob's.

Why?

Was it Cassie?

Was it—

Yacob's palm pressed gently to Wendy's. "The temple of the Lord is within us all."

Golden light swelled around him, bright enough to hurt. Wendy blinked through tears and the tide of light washed Yacob away.

He was gone.

Deep mists in her memory cleared as the fog on the mountain lifted. The church came to her—faces stepping out of

Wendy's repression like they'd been watching her from behind a curtain. Father Linton. Mrs. Corley. Mr. Munson. Old Lady Hunts with the mints. Hands offering coats in winter, cans of soup, invitations to meals. Kindness Wendy's mother had called judgment.

Wendy had never felt judged there.

Only loved.

And when her mother left Yacob for some addict, Wendy had cried until her throat split because the only safe place she'd known had disappeared.

"Don't go," Wendy whispered, and the words fell useless onto Yacob's empty platter.

She jerked in the chair as if waking from a nightmare, and for a second the restraints were gone and her body remembered how to move.

The Stranger lifted the needle.

"You can join him," he offered, voice soft as a pillow. "End the suffering. Be safe."

Wendy's gut clenched. The sickness swelled like a wave. Her plate steamed in front of her, Grace bubbling and brown and sweetly toxic. It promised numbness. It promised quiet.

It promised a way out.

She could be with Yacob.

Be safe.

"She's too defiant," Mr. Dream said, amused.

The Stranger's head snapped toward him. The needle flicked up—sharp, fast—aimed at an eye, a threat made elegant.

Defiance.

The word lit something in Wendy that wasn't Grace and wasn't the growth.

Father Linton's voice rang in her memory: *God doesn't want you on your knees all day. He gave you feet.*

Pray. Stand. Fight.

Fight for the Kingdom of God to be here! Now! Not some place after you die. Make this world Heaven—don't sit around and wait for it to be delivered. Make it happen!

Yacob hadn't wanted her weak.

He wanted her to fight. Taught her how to do it.

He wanted her alive.

Wendy wiped her cheeks with the back of her hand. Her face settled. Not calm—steel.

Cassie clapped once, eager and bright, like she could feel the shift.

Wendy looked at Mr. Dream—Noah—suit and yellow teeth, divinity stripped down to a man who needed people to believe.

And she laughed.

Not hysterical. Not broken.

Dismissive.

Defiant.

"You are no God," Wendy said.

Mr. Dream returned her laugh with his own.

EIGHTEEN

"Would you know God if you saw him?" Mr. Dream asked.

Wendy's laugh came out sharp and ugly.

God was the warmth of hot chocolate after the Christmas pageant. God was Mrs. Corley's hand on the soccer ball, rolling it back to Wendy and saying, *Perfect practice makes perfect.* God was soup left on a doorstep. Coats in winter. A room that smelled like soap.

The Sleep House had been none of that. It didn't have a caring preacher but a shut-in with lights and rules, calling himself holy while people rotted on his floor.

Wendy stared at the man in the suit. The man she used to kneel for. "Why are you so hideous?"

Mr. Dream shrugged and smiled. He held his syringe like a fork and prodded the blister on his platter.

The thing was alive—swollen black skin, a seam split and weeping. Every careful poke made the membrane shiver. The infected stench leaked out, again bringing the rotten fruit to mind.

"I speak plainly now," Mr. Dream said. "You have ascended. You're no longer my faithful."

Wendy's jaw clenched. "I was never your anything."

"You were not my peer," he snapped. Candlelight blazed in his eyes. "You crawled to me broken. I gave you shelter. I demanded obedience. I kept others from touching you." He jabbed the blister again, slow. "And what did you do?"

The blister popped.

Thick pus bulged out, pale green and glossy. It slumped onto the silver platter in heavy ropes. The smell grabbed her throat, choked her, made her eyes water. It stomped her gut, making her gag, her head spin.

"Oh, God," she groaned, covering her mouth to hold the little in her back.

"You asked questions," Mr. Dream said, pleased.

"What god fears the questions of a mortal?" Wendy hissed. "No god. You are no god."

Mr. Dream set the syringe down and leaned toward her, smile thin. "I didn't fear them. I hated them." He tapped the table once, like punctuation. "Doubt devours. Doubt takes root. It's an infection you can't excise. You can only let it spread—or burn everything around it."

Wendy remembered the question—the one that cast her down like a fallen angel.

She forced it out again, tasting old fear. "Why can't you leave the Sleep House?"

For a heartbeat, Mr. Dream's face went still.

Not anger.

Not laughter.

Stillness.

Then rage flooded back in. "That justified me being cast down?" Wendy pressed. "That justified Cassie dying?"

Cassie didn't move.

Mr. Dream's gaze slid toward the Stranger—just a flicker, a check—and something in the air tightened. The Stranger's smile thinned, warning. Mr. Dream waved it away like shooing a fly.

"You think that's a simple question," Mr. Dream said. "We all have a past."

His mouth twitched. "But you…" He let the word hang, savoring it. "You were blessed to forget."

Wendy's skin prickled.

Mr. Dream's eyes sharpened, as if he'd almost said more and caught himself. "You think your life was bleak." His voice softened into something crueler than shouting. "Sister, you cannot fathom Hell."

"So, you keep people in it!" Wendy shouted.

"The Sleep House isn't Hell," Mr. Dream corrected, offended. "It's…mercy. For most." He gestured around the table as if this nightmare were proof of his generosity. "To most, I'm the last stop. The only place left."

Then his gaze slid back to Wendy and hardened.

"But you poisoned us."

Wendy went cold.

Mr. Dream's smile returned. "I should never have let you stay. You were poison. You knew it then. You know it now." His finger stabbed across the table toward Yacob's empty chair as if the air still held him. "That's why you never went back."

"No," Wendy said.

"That's why you killed your mother," Mr. Dream continued, voice bright with certainty.

"No!"

"That's why everyone kept away from you in the Sleep House—"

"No!"

"That's why only the naïve came close and you—"

Wendy slammed her palm down. Silver platters jumped. Domes rang like bells.

"And that's why you killed her," Mr. Dream snapped, stabbing a finger at Cassie. "You infected her with your rot and now—"

Cassie lifted her eyes.

Not to Wendy.

To Mr. Dream.

Mr. Dream's words died in his throat.

The silence was a blade.

Wendy took it. "You killed her," she screamed, leaning over her own platter. Heat breathed up at her—Grace bubbling brown and chemical-sweet. Her body leaned toward it without permission. "You did this!"

Mr. Dream shot to his feet. "She died because she stayed with you!" he roared back, face red, spit shining. "You could've cast her away. You could've left. You could've done *anything*—anything—to save her and what did you do? What!"

The answer boiled in Wendy like vomit.

She saw herself under the stairs, curled around the lunchbox, hoarding baggies, counting them like they were days of life. Saving. Saving. Saving.

Waiting.

For what?

Cassie had waited with her.

Cassie—soft, new to suffering, not yet calcified, not yet stone. Cassie who wanted to hold and be held and didn't ask for anything else.

Wendy's voice came out small. "I did nothing."

The fire that had held her upright burned out.

"I did nothing," she confessed. Her voice caught, stumbled over the realization.

Mr. Dream's hands hit the table.

Pus splashed up in milky green drops and speckled his suit. The fabric hissed where it landed, eating through like acid. He struck again. Again. Each slam sprayed more rot.

Wendy shrank from the stench—chemical, infected, burning. In her soul, she ached – the soreness of doing nothing, of letting Cassie die. It hollowed her out. Melting her as Mr. Dream began to melt.

His skin began to sag.

The acid devoured him.

His cheeks liquefied. His lips drooped, sliding off his face in soft strips. His eyes bulged and then drooled down what remained, as if even his skull couldn't hold him together.

"God was listening," he gurgled, voice deepening into something inhuman, "but you weren't talking. You weren't wanting." He slammed the table again. "You did nothing to save her. And less to save yourself."

His glossy white shoes—those shoes Wendy had kissed and bowed to—collapsed into a hissing puddle. Blood swirled through creamy green goo on the floor.

Then Mr. Dream was gone.

Not vanished.

Dissolved.

Wendy folded forward onto the table, face in her arms, and sobbed. Her ribs strained to hold the sorrow in, the absolute failure swelling within her. "I did nothing," she screamed into her sleeves. The words came out warped by withdrawal, by grief, by the truth clawing at her throat.

Behind her eyelids, Cassie's last days replayed in the murky bleakness of the Sleep House.

Cassie shaking, bugs in her skin, buzzing filling her world. Wendy held her, rocking her and giving her just enough Grace to keep her close—because Wendy needed to be needed.

When Cassie finally snapped and ran into the street, Wendy didn't get up.

Tires screeched stop.

Screams erupted.

Silence.

Tires screeched to flee.

Silence.

Wendy held the last baggie of Grace and listened for Cassie to come back.

When she didn't return, Wendy took a pinky of Grace to her gums and slept, numb, and nothing for days.

Wendy heard about Cassie's death—overheard it like gossip—because Wendy was too high to move, too high to care, too high to do anything but let the world happen without her.

The bugs woke under Wendy's skin now, ants nibbling at muscle and bone, skittering toward the Stranger's empty needle like they knew the fastest escape.

The Stranger held the needle out to her. "The final course is the hardest."

Wendy lifted her head, eyes burning. "I can't," she whispered. Snot ran. Drool slid. She hated herself for every sound her body made. "I can't."

The needle was right there.

The Grace on her plate boiled and breathed. Her tears and snot dripped into it, mixing with the toxic heat.

One stab and she'd feel the burst of light, then quiet. Dreamless. Numbness.

Wendy reached.

Cassie's hand covered hers.

Warm. Solid.

Wendy froze.

Cassie shook her head and smiled like nothing bad had ever happened.

"You're almost there," Cassie said.

Wendy sobbed harder. "Please. I can't—I just—I can't—"

Wendy reached again.

Cassie pressed her hand down again, gentle as prayer.

Then Cassie guided Wendy's hand toward Cassie's platter.

Wendy's eyes fell to it.

It could have been ashes.

A dagger.

A wound.

But what was there…it was as horrible as it was fitting.

It was nothing.

NINETEEN

"Oh, Wendy," Cassie said softly, and smiled. "You look terrible."

That was the same thing she'd say when the sickness had Wendy and Wendy couldn't stop shaking, couldn't stop sweating, couldn't stop begging for death to come. Only Cassie's light helped her through those horrible dark times.

But now, Cassie didn't glow.

Not the way Wendy remembered. Not the way Cassie had in the Library—mousy brown hair, crooked grin, she glowed, a beacon in a rotten place.

Here, Cassie filled the room. Her presence flattened the air between them. The Stranger stared at her unblinking, just like the candles, just like Wendy.

Her dress didn't belong in a cave. Black gown, bare shoulders with tan lines like she'd walked straight off a beach and into this nightmare. Her skin looked clean. Alive. Her smile was too young, too fresh for someone who endured the Sleep House.

Wendy's throat worked, dry and sore.

"Why don't you have anything?" Wendy forced herself to look at the empty platter. Emptiness should have been relief. Instead, it made her skin crawl.

Cassie's gaze moved—not to her own plate, but across the table to the empty chair where Yacob had been, and the space where her mother's dust had scattered, and the slick puddle where Mr. Dream had dissolved.

"They had what you took," Cassie said quietly. She motioned to Yacob and her mother's empty platters, then to her own and Mr. Dream's. "We have what you gave."

"That's not true," Wendy blurted. Panic rose too fast. "I loved you."

Cassie's smile held for a second too long. Then it softened— pity, gentle and poisonous.

"You tried," Cassie said, and reached across the table.

Her hand closed around Wendy's.

Warm.

Not mist. Not memory.

Warmth sank into Wendy's skin, starved for something good to fill her. Something to pour into the chasm left by her mother, Yacob, and Mr. Dream. But her touch was only a reminder of what had been cut out, carved away.

"You tried," Cassie repeated. "But it's hard to give what you've never been taught how to have."

Wendy swallowed. "I—"

Cassie didn't let her hide inside the word.

"You didn't even come see if I was dead," Cassie said, still gentle. Still holding Wendy's hand, her thumb gently rubbing Wendy's.

Wendy flinched. The sentence bit her heart, grinding, gnawing. "I—I couldn't move."

"I know." Cassie lowered herself to meet Wendy's empty stare. Her eyes were familiar. Almost kind. "You took the last hit."

Wendy's stomach clenched.

"The lunchbox," Cassie said. Her voice was soft the way people get soft when they're about to be cruel. "You said it was empty."

Wendy tried to pull her hand away. Cassie didn't tighten her grip. She didn't have to. Wendy's muscles couldn't fight a kind grip, no more than a crushing one.

"That hit would've saved me," Cassie whispered. "One more day. One more hour. Long enough." She gave Wendy a small, sad smile. "If you loved me, you would've given it to me."

Wendy's eyes burned. "I did love you."

Cassie's smile didn't change, but something behind it sharpened.

"Actually," Cassie said, conversational, "if you loved me, you would've left when I asked."

Wendy saw it—Cassie in the Library, voice shaking with hope, begging Wendy to take her out. Wendy pressing Grace into Cassie's mouth instead. Wendy choosing numbness over motion because numbness was the only safety she trusted.

After that night, Cassie asked no more.

Wendy's chest tightened until breathing hurt. "I'm sorry."

Cassie cradled Wendy's hands in both of hers, warm and steady. "I know," she said. "I know you are."

A beat passed.

Cassie waited.

Not for apology. Not really.

For something else.

For a sentence Wendy couldn't find.

Wendy didn't know what it was—only that the absence of it made Cassie's pity heavier.

Cassie's voice shifted, lightening like she was changing the subject. "Do you remember telling me about church?" she asked. Her smile came back, bright and eager in a way that made Wendy's skin prickle. "I always thought you'd take me there one day."

Wendy jerked back in her chair. "Cassie—"

Cassie's eyes held her, unblinking. "No. Of course you don't remember that," Cassie said, and her voice was still kind, which made it worse. "But why did you take the word of addicts over seeing for yourself?"

Wendy couldn't speak.

Shame bloomed in her. Hot. Filling the emptiness. Spinning fast, chaotically teetering. Tumbling over and over until it shattered, breaking into shards of fear—fear that Cassie saw Wendy as she truly was.

A monster.

Cassie watched it happen with the patience of someone who knew exactly where Wendy would fall.

"Tell me," Cassie said softly. "What did you give me?"

Wendy's mind spiraled. The familiar descent—self-loathing, numbness, the urge to disappear into anything that wasn't thinking. Sex. Drugs. Alcohol. Any distraction.

It distracted her from the spiral.

From—

Wendy's throat tightened.

From the Spiral.

Cassie clicked her tongue once, sharp and practiced, and Wendy's attention snapped back like a leash.

"I begged you to leave," Cassie said. "We could have gone—"

"I did love you," Wendy whispered. "The best I knew how."

Cassie froze.

Then slowly, she reached up and slid a chain from her neck.

Gold links clinked softly as they hit the plate.

A pendant dropped into the candlelight.

Stone. White marble shot through with black veins that pulsed, writhed, as if the rock had a heartbeat trapped inside it.

A spiral.

Wendy's vision tunneled.

The pendant hummed—low, almost inaudible—and the hum didn't just touch her ears. It pressed behind her eyes. It vibrated in her teeth. The room tilted, not from sickness but from recognition she couldn't place.

Not a dream.

Not memory exactly.

Something older than both.

Cassie stood, slow, controlled. "My sweet Wendy," she said, and her voice softened into something that sounded like mercy. "You can't love. You can only be numb."

Wendy's stomach rolled. "That's not—"

Cassie lifted a finger. "It's okay," she said, and the words were a blanket with hooks. "You are broken." Each word latching into her flesh, tugging as she pulled away, holding her steadfast for more suffering.

Cassie leaned closer across, eyes bright with a private certainty. "And you'll stay broken until you fix the one thing you keep refusing to look at."

Wendy's breath hitched.

Forgiveness.

That's what Wendy heard. That's what Wendy needed. Cassie's forgiveness, Yacob's forgiveness, God's—real God's forgiveness. Something to scrub the rot out.

But Cassie's gaze flicked to the pendant, and Wendy felt the hum again, deeper.

"What do you even remember?" Cassie asked, voice almost curious. "Before the Sleep House. Before the stairs. Before the nothing." Cassie's smile softened as if she pitied Wendy for being small. "Do you remember *living*?"

Wendy's mind grabbed for images and found flashes: a tall shape like a tower against lightning; a narrow stair; heat in her palms; the word *'again'* spoken the way Yacob used to say it when she threw a punch wrong—

Tower?

The word stung, a deep bruise splintering her bones.

Why?

Cassie watched Wendy's eyes change and smiled. A hint of recognition flared, then her hope faded.

"You're terrified of remembering," Cassie whispered. "Because if you remember, you'll have to become someone again."

Cassie walked behind Wendy, placing her hands on her shoulders. Wendy reached up, caressed one hand, again feeling the warmth. Cassie's breath wound through Wendy's neck hairs in a humid gasp.

Wendy's voice came out broken. "Are you—" She swallowed. "Are you alive?"

The question felt impossible as it left her.

Cassie's hand was warm.

Cassie's grip was real.

No one else here felt real.

From somewhere in the room—not from the candles, not from the empty chairs—something shifted.

A shadow stood up without standing.

Wendy's skin prickled. The Stranger. Not fully a body, not fully a thought—presence gathering in the corner of her vision.

"Your time is up," the Stranger said.

Cassie turned her head slightly, her eyes sharpening. Her smile vanished. A snarl flashed—quick, bestial.

"I decide when my time is up," Cassie said.

The Stranger sat back down.

Not in anger.

In fear.

Wendy felt it—felt the way his presence shrank from Cassie's voice.

When her eyes met Wendy's, Cassie's smile returned, sweet as poison. "Don't go back to the Sleep House," she said. "If you're going to die…" she nodded toward the spiral pendant on the plate, "…at least die in the light."

"Do you want me to die?" Wendy whispered. "Is that justice?" Her throat tightened around the old word. "What about forgiveness?"

Cassie laughed softly, almost indulgent.

Wendy stiffened. Every nerve lit up. Cassie leaned close. Her breath touched Wendy's ear—hot, intimate, too close.

"You brought me to the Craft," Cassie whispered. The word landed heavy, familiar, wrong. "And even if you don't remember who you are…" Cassie's lips brushed Wendy's hair as she spoke, a deliberate cruelty. "I do."

Wendy shook, trying to turn, but her body moved too slow.

"You made me," Cassie said, voice velvet-smooth. "You are my creator."

Wendy's heart hammered. "Cassie—please—"

Cassie's whisper sharpened. "Creators don't beg their creations for forgiveness."

Wendy went cold.

She couldn't hold the room together anymore. She could only hold onto the one bright fact:

Cassie might be alive.

Cassie might be here.

Forgiveness might exist.

"I'll find you," Wendy said, desperate. "I'll make it right."

Cassie's hand touched Wendy's shoulder—light, almost affectionate.

Then it was gone.

No footsteps.

Just absence.

Was she ever there?

Wendy's breath shook.

The spiral pendant still lay on Cassie's platter.

Real.

Waiting.

Wendy picked it up.

The stone was cold—too heavy to be only stone—and it hummed against her skin like a slow drum. The black veins inside it seemed to shift as if they were alive.

She slipped the chain over her head and let the pendant settle against her chest.

Against her heart.

Warmth spread—not comfort. Power. Pressure. A low thrum that made her teeth ache.

At the table:

Her mother was gone.

Yacob was gone.

Mr. Dream's rot had puddled and cooled.

No one else had left anything behind.

Because none of them had been real.

Wendy's mouth went dry.

Only Cassie.

And now the Stranger again—standing, walking to Wendy in a slow swagger. He sat on the table's edge, placing the key and the needle in front of Wendy.

The needle gleamed.

The key sat dull and ordinary.

The choice waited between them like a held breath.

It was time to finish this feast.

TWENTY

"Choose," the Stranger said.

Wendy didn't hesitate.

She grabbed the key.

Rust scraped her fingertips—flaking iron biting under her nails—and the sensation sent a sharp echo up her arm, a phantom sting blooming along old needle tracks. Pain rippled and faded under the bigger fact swelling in her chest:

She wasn't lost.

There was a door.

There was a way out.

Cassie was alive.

Cassie hadn't fallen apart like her mother. Hadn't dissolved like Mr. Dream. Cassie's hand had been warm. Real. Cassie had left the pendant behind like proof.

Wendy rose from the chair, legs shaking. The table held her up. Quivering arms trembled. Her feet screamed with every step, but she pulled herself along the table to escape. The platters were gone. The chairs, too—vanishing…if they ever existed.

Only the door remained.

Wendy pushed herself to it. She shoved the key into the lock.

Rust squealed.

"Before you open it," the Stranger called.

Wendy froze, key half-turned.

Behind her, the Stranger rolled his shoulders then pushed his sleeves up as if the real work were now about to begin. But he wasn't pushing up his sleeves, he was slicing open his forearms. His razor-sharp pinky broke the flesh releasing not blood, but black smoke.

The Stranger drew the nail up his arm, to his chest, to his throat, unzipping his body to release the smog within.

The human shape peeled away without sound. A false costume falling off.

Under it stood something with onyx flesh, wreathed in quivering smoke. Muscles flexed, stretching and straining to break through his skin. A white mask covered its face—two thin slits where eyes should be, no nose, no mouth.

The gap under her ribs, where the growth that whispered for years, now empty, burned. It pulsed. It writhed. Her eyes met The Stranger's eyes, watching him breathe, feeling the coiling and uncoiling within her matching the rise and fall of his shoulders.

The Stranger.

The growth.

The thing that had lived under Wendy's ribs her whole life in the Sleep House.

"If you walk through that door," it said, voice smooth with warning, "I won't be with you to hide what you've forgotten."

Wendy's breath caught.

The fog in her mind cleared, burned off in the heat of The Stranger's cruelty.

Images slammed into her in strobing bursts—too fast to hold, too sharp to be dreams.

Her mother in a motel bathtub, skin gray, smile small and satisfied. Dead.

Yacob's arms around her—strong and warm—crying into her hair. Her mother ripping her away, throwing her into a car as the addict boyfriend stared, drooling over her.

A needle in her hand. Heroin glinting like honey.

A motel bed. A man pointing. A camera. A clown mask slipping over a face.

A woman without a face holding out a cookie in a forest—

Wendy's stomach rolled. Her throat closed.

"No." The word scraped out.

Not that image. Not that image!

More came.

They weren't memories rising. They were *released*—the dam cracked. They poured through.

Wendy hit the floor, key still in her fist, and screamed.

"Stop!" she begged. "No more—"

The Stranger tilted his head to the music of her horror. Delight tightened the air around him. He watched her squirm the way he had always watched—from inside her, whispering, coiling, patient.

Then he looked down at a speck of grime under his claw like Wendy's agony had already gotten boring.

"Well," he said lightly, "I can't help you with what's coming."

Wendy vomited.

Water and milky protein drink splattered out, hot and sour. She fell into it. Her cheek splashing into the puddle. Her cheek pressing to the slimy wet floor, mouth open and gagging.

The shakes hit.

Not the usual tremors.

This was a full-body seizure of need, muscles twisting driving rusty screws into her nerves—turning tighter, tighter, tighter—until her teeth jittered in her skull.

Wendy tried to scream but only a thin, animal whine came out.

The Stranger laughed.

"Oh, so sick," he mocked. "I was holding that back too. I'm considerate."

He drifted closer, smoke billowing into a cloak behind him.

"Consider what got you here," he purred.

Wendy stiffened.

The voice—*the voice*—the one that had always been in the back of her head, telling her she was filthy, telling her she deserved every hand that hit her, telling her numbness was mercy.

She hadn't recognized it because she couldn't remember a time without it.

The growth inside her had always sounded like truth.

The Stranger was the demon inside her.

The Stranger was what she ran from. Horn said *what she ran from would find her here*, and he did. He found her. And now he wasn't content with tormenting her mind, or body, or soul – he wanted to torture every piece of her.

He smiled behind a mouthless mask. "Go on," he said. "Use the key. Walk out. Start your new life."

Then he paused, drifting his attention to the table that wasn't there anymore, the feast that might have never been.

"Unless," he murmured, and the word curled through Wendy like smoke, "you'd prefer something easier."

A needle dangled from his fingertips.

Empty.

Waiting.

"Something that takes it all away," he whispered. "No memories. No pain. No you." He swooped down, her silver platter fizzling into existence in his hand. He placed it before her. The boiling Grace still hot. Still sizzling with sweet toxic waste smells and choking poisonous flavors.

Wendy dry-heaved.

Nothing came out, but the convulsion didn't stop. Her throat clenched and clenched, trying to expel a meal that wasn't there. Her vision tunneled. Pressure built behind her eyes, and built. She heaved harder. Her eyes bulged. Ready to pop. But they didn't. Each heave strained to hold them in her skull.

The Stranger hovered above her, laughing softly, letting the torment linger.

The needle hung close enough that Wendy could smell it— melted plastic and infected blood.

Wendy wanted it to fall.

Wanted it to split her skin and flood her with the old nothing. Wanted to do what her mother had done: escape.

But the Stranger made a mistake.

It had dragged Yacob into this room.

And Yacob had planted something in Wendy that didn't rot.

A mop, he'd said. *God gave us free will to muck things up. And God gave us a mop to clean it up. The mop's called…*

Faith.

Wendy's hands shook so hard she couldn't keep hold of the key. She caught it with both palms, pressing it between them like prayer, and crawled to the lock on her knees.

Every muscle seized. Every breath tore. Her feet were ruined. Her stomach empty. Her mind full of knives.

But the key was real.

Wendy forced it into the lock.

Her jaw chattered. "I can find forgiveness," she rasped.

The Stranger's laugh softened. "From others? Sure." It leaned down, voice intimate. "But what about from yourself?"

The key slipped from Wendy's fingers and clattered to the floor.

For a second she couldn't move. Couldn't breathe.

Forgive herself?

The thought was worse than the memories.

Because everything she'd survived had taught her the same lie: it was her fault.

Wendy swallowed hard, grabbed the key again, and shoved it into the lock.

"God will forgive me," she said, not because she believed it, but because Yacob believed it. "Who am I to question Him?"

She turned the key.

The lock gave.

The door swung open.

Cold mountain air slammed into the room like mercy. It blew the melted-plastic stink out of Wendy's nose and replaced it with pine and rain and thin, clean cold.

A brown-cloaked figure rushed in.

Horn.

"Aspirant Wendy!" he shouted—her name hitting the air like a command.

She collapsed over the threshold, clawing at dirt with broken fingers like she could drag herself toward Cassie, toward light, toward anything that wasn't the tunnel.

The Stranger hissed.

Horn replied with an ancient word, a powerful word. The demon flickered like static, smoke tearing in jagged strips. It recoiled—shuddering—then Horn screamed the word again, shouting it at The Stranger.

The demon screamed in pain, fizzled, then phased out of reality with a crackling pop, leaving only foul stink hanging in the air.

Horn hauled Wendy away from the vomit pool, rolling her onto her side. "We didn't think you made it," he said, breath harsh. He shoved a water bottle to her lips. "Drink. Slow."

Wendy's throat gulped on instinct, finally realizing how dry she was. Hunger tore through her belly. Shivers tore through her limbs.

"How are you still alive?" Horn gasped. "I thought you… died, weeks ago."

"How… long…" she tried. How could he have thought she died weeks ago? Hadn't it only been hours? Days at most…

Horn's face tightened. "Three weeks."

The words didn't fit in Wendy's head.

A monk in a white cloak rushed in with an EMT kit, fingers fast and practiced. He checked her pulse, her eyes, her breathing.

Horn kept his arms around Wendy as if letting go would make her vanish. "We saw the readings," he said, voice tight. "We thought you were dead. Then the energy readings spiked and we—well, I didn't know what it meant. I've never seen anything like that. Then the door opened just as we—" He stared at her like she was a miracle he didn't trust. "I don't…You didn't have enough supplies. The pills—"

Wendy's hand twitched weakly against Horn's sleeve.

"Faith," she whispered. "God wouldn't let me fail."

Horn went still.

His breath hitched. He held the silence while the EMTs worked. Then a laugh broke out of him—too loud, too sharp, wrong for this moment. Not joy.

Revelation.

"Faith," he repeated, like he'd just tasted a word that changed everything. He cradled Wendy tighter. "Faith…" His eyes went distant, calculating. "The Order needs this. Needs… you."

The EMT fitted an oxygen mask over her face. The world hissed as air fed into her lungs.

A monk stepped in with a needle.

Wendy didn't feel the injection.

Only the quiet dark sliding over her.

Dreamless.

TWENTY-ONE

Wendy lifted her head to see Horn. He sat in a chair across for her, smiling.

"Welcome back," he said and came to her bedside. He sat near her feet, keeping clear of the nurse moving around the bed.

This room was pretending to be a hospital.

The walls were a calming green. Machines blinked and beeped beside her bed. People in white cloaks moved with practiced quiet, red crosses stitched on their chests to reassure.

The air smelled like antiseptic and clean nothing.

The room *sounded* like safety.

But the window was wrong.

A city Wendy didn't recognize—rooftops and streetlights and a strip of water catching the last of the day stretched out her window. The sun was setting, warm and gold, but something in it bothered her. The light didn't match what her body remembered. It felt…tilted. Like it was shining from a direction it shouldn't.

Wendy lay still and listened to herself.

No bugs under her skin.

No crawling electricity in her nerves.

The withdrawal had loosened its grip. Her body was quiet for the first time in what felt like a lifetime.

A needle hovered at the edge of her vision.

A nurse—young, steady hands—checked the monitor and then Wendy's pulse. She held a syringe filled with clear liquid.

"This will help with the pain," the nurse said, softly, calm reassurance.

Wendy's feet throbbed under the blanket, shredded and swollen. Her calves ached from the mountain. Her joints felt bruised down to bone.

"No." Wendy's eyes locked on the needle. "I don't need it."

The nurse paused and looked to Horn.

He shrugged as if to say, *her call.* Horn stood, joining another monk by the door. The other man stood with a relaxed posture Wendy didn't trust.

"I'd rather feel it," Wendy said. Her voice scraped, but it was hers. "I've been feeling nothing too long."

Horn watched her for a beat, then flicked two fingers to dismiss.

The nurse lowered the syringe and stepped back.

Horn moved closer to the bed, careful not to crowd. "This is a safe place," he said. "No demons can reach you here."

Wendy's throat tightened. She'd been told places were safe before. That word, *safe*, had teeth.

"Where is here?" she asked.

The man lingering at the doorway left.

Outside her door, voices drifted by—mundane conversation, laughter, someone complaining about a bad cup of coffee. Not whispered. Not fearful. Life happening without checking corners.

The Sleep House had never sounded like this.

Horn answered as if he'd been waiting for the question. "You're with the Sylvan Order," he said. "Annapolis, Maryland."

The words didn't fit. A place name from a life Wendy didn't remember.

"Think of us like a hospital for the soul," Horn added. He gave a small, almost genuine smile. "When you're better, you can go home."

Wendy's mouth went dry.

Of course he said that.

Mr. Dream had said you could always leave too—because they knew you had nowhere else to go. Just like Horn knew the same.

Horn's gaze held hers like he could see the thought. "Rest," he said, and the word came out less like comfort and more like instruction. "For those who survive what you survived… recovery takes time."

Wendy swallowed. "On the mountain," she said, "you were surprised by the number you captured." Her voice steadied as she spoke. "Who were they? Why were they trying to get me?"

Horn's expression tightened—just a flicker. Calculation. Then he decided what to give her.

"Those weren't people," he said. "They were demons."

Wendy didn't blink.

Horn continued anyway. "Some demons cling to people. Some hunt. Sometimes we have to clear them away so an aspirant can face the master."

"The master?" Wendy echoed.

Horn didn't answer.

"But you said I had… so many," Wendy pressed. "Why?"

Horn's eyes went distant for a heartbeat, like he'd stepped around his own thoughts. "Most people have one internal demon," he said, voice controlled. "And a handful outside— three, five—things that hang over them. They don't even know what they are. We do."

His gaze returned to Wendy. "You had just over thirty."

Wendy felt her stomach drop.

Horn's voice went quieter. "Whatever was inside you must have been powerful to draw that many."

Wendy remembered smoke. The mask. The voice that had lived under her ribs for years. The needle dangling.

"It's gone now," Horn said, almost satisfied. "Whatever was inside you, it's gone."

Wendy's hand moved under the blanket, fingers tracing the spiral pendant at her chest—cold stone, heavy enough to feel like truth.

"Then why can I still feel it?" she asked.

But could she feel it? Was it the pendant sitting on her chest or…The Stranger?

Horn shook his head once. "The demon can be gone," he said, "and still leave scars." He nodded toward her feet as if to make the metaphor physical.

He continued, "The past is the past. It leaves the door open if you don't guard it." He started toward the exit. The other people left but he lingered. "We keep the door shut," he said, and his tone made it sound less like a promise and more like a war.

Before he stepped out, he looked back over his shoulder. "But any demon that turns an eye to you will think twice."

"Why?" Wendy asked, hating the need for an answer. Questions…felt different here. Allowed.

"The demons talk. They know when they've lost. They're lazy and won't try to conquer a hard ass like you." He laughed. "Now get some rest. I'll be back tomorrow."

Then he was gone, leaving the door to click softly behind him.

Wendy lay awake anyway.

The machines beeped. The antiseptic smell sat on her tongue. The room tried to lull her, but her mind wouldn't let it.

A horror movie of memories played behind her eyes.

BBQ chicken at church.

Her mother's voice telling her to hide under the bed when someone knocked.

Yacob's hands guiding hers in prayer.

A boyfriend with wild eyes insisting he could fly, trying to drag Wendy to the edge with him.

And then the woman without a face in the woods—gardening, as if it were normal. Cookies warm in an oven that wasn't electric, a wood stove breathing heat into the room—

"No," Wendy whispered into the pillow. "Not that one."

The memory backed away, polite as a predator choosing to wait.

Most of the memories were childhood, then the faceless woman, then blank.

Then the Sleep House.

Nothing in between.

A stretch of her life missing like someone had cut the film.

Wendy's chest tightened around one thought that kept pushing forward like a tongue against a sore tooth:

Cassie.

Was Cassie alive?

Or was the demon—gone or not—still taunting her with hope?

Wendy's fingers found the spiral pendant again.

She traced the ridges, the curve winding inward to a single point.

Proof.

Cassie had left it.

Cassie was real.

Forgiveness existed in the living.

And if Wendy could get Cassie's forgiveness… maybe she could learn how to stop hating herself long enough to breathe.

Wendy closed her eyes.

Cassie's crooked smile hovered behind her lids.

A lullaby drifted up from the Sleep House—rainbows, sunshine, stars—sweet enough to be dangerous. Wendy finally fell asleep.

Her dream, the one she had in the shed, came again. She killed Mr. Dream. She killed the monks. She stood over their fallen bodies cackling. Her lungs strained to make space for the joy filling her from all the death. All the destruction. And under her ribs, she found the hot, molten coil that gave her space for all this - to be who she truly was meant to be.

She slept uneasy, tormented by what the mountain left behind.

EPILOGUE

"Enter," the ancient man didn't rise from his writing. He hunched over the wooden desk that might have been as old as him, but it was doubtful. These days it didn't feel like much was as old as he, especially in the mornings when his tendons creaked like weathered bamboo.

"Arch Druid Raskins, you summoned me?" Acolyte Horn entered the study.

Raskins preferred silent candlelight to the constant hum of the new lights. They cast a greenish hue to everything, sickly and pale compared to the warm life of candles. And wasn't the Sylvan Order a place of life? Yet the new lights are easier, simply flip a switch. No need to light and extinguish. But some tasks, like journaling are best when accompanied with chores such as maintaining your light, your ink, your thoughts. He dipped his quill and returned to his journal's tome.

"I heard you found an interesting specimen?"

"Arch Druid?"

"The lady you took to the mountain. I heard she survived, and long beyond her ration supply." Raskins placed his quill down and scooted his chair back. The legs stuttered against the stone floor. "I have heard that you brought her back here for treatment."

"Yes, Arch Druid. That seemed the most prudent action." Horn replied.

"Bringing her here or taking her to the mountain to begin with?" Raskins reclined and steepled his fingers. The chair squeaked under his slight frame.

Horn stiffened at the question.

"Ascension has not been forbidden—"

"But it has been dismissed as a ritual of the old way," Raskins interrupted. "We are evolving Acolyte. The old ways are not the future of the Sylvan Order."

Horn sucked in a sharp breath. His lips parted, but then he lowered his head and closed his mouth.

"You have a bright future in the Order. We need men of focus and dedication such as yourself, but we must all evolve. If we only accepted those who could thrive in Ascension, we'd be very few in number to face the enemy," Raskins said.

Horn nodded.

"Now, tell me of this woman. Do you believe her to be up to the life of the Order?"

Horn kept his head down and answered, "Yes. She's, she's

different. I don't know where she was before the Sleep House, neither does she."

"And Noah? What does he say?"

"He only said she entered the Sleep House on her own accord. He didn't know where she came from either."

"She simply showed up in that place?" Raskins harrumphed. "Unlikely. No one wanders by and sees relief in that refuse."

Horn said, "She had an army of demons stalking her. We've never seen so many stalking a single person."

"Do you have a theory on why?" Raskins leaned forward. His brow furrowed with interest as his chair squeaked and shifted closer to Horn.

"That many demons," Horn considered, "that is not an accidental collection. They didn't just find her. They were looking for her."

"Or, looking for the demon within her." Raskins corrected.

"And that is why I took her to the mountain. Demons cannot hide on sacred ground," Horn's explanation bordered on rationalization instead of sticking to the facts.

Raskins raised his hand to stop this thread.

"To be sought by demons," Raskins paused, thoughts connecting in his old mind as quickly as they did in his youth. Of all the things failing in his old age, his mind was not one. "Has she ever left this realm?"

Horn shrugged, "I don't know. But I assume so. I think she could have the answers we're seeking. Maybe the knowledge to turn the tide in our war. She's different."

Raskins nodded slowly. "Let us learn what we can from this new guest. She will need to be approved by the Council as all are. Keep this one on a short leash. I fear that one who drew the attention of so much evil, will surely bring the wicked into our home."

Horn agreed. "Her faith is strong. I believe she will thrive here."

Raskins returned to his journal considering the wickedness this woman could bring into their Order. He could excise her now, not give the infection a moment to root—but then what would Horn do in response? He and his followers, those who want the Order to be what it once was, would they object? Would rejecting this woman create the moment Horn seeks to rally those who seek to return to the old ways?

"You are excused Acolyte Horn," Raskins said.

"Yes, Arch Druid." Horn went to the door.

"And Acolyte," Raskins added, "the Ritual of Ascension is no longer something we observe. Do not return to the mountain with candidates."

Silence. Had Horn already left? No, the door creaked. He stood at the exit considering his words. But then only said, "Yes, Arch Druid." He closed the door and left.

Regret swelled in Raskins as the door clicked closed. This was the wrong decision. The men who came in with Horn talked of this woman, this Wendy, as if she were a warrior. Her ascent had already become storied and legends fester without being controlled. But control was gone. Horn's men were infected with her story and how many others have they infected now?

This woman, Wendy, was poison.

But what could be done?

To have so many demons seeking her—there was only one explanation—she had been to the realm of the demons and returned. Why was she here in this realm?

What ruin will she bring?

What ruin will she bring upon the Order?

THE END

Keep reading for a sneak peek at Faith & Deed Book II: THE ORDER.

BOOK 2
THE ORDER

I hope you enjoy this special sneak peek at THE ORDER, the next story in the Faith & Deed series. The story begins where *Ascension* ends with Wendy in the hospital that isn't quite a hospital. In the second book, we dive deep into the mysterious Sylvan Order, and discover the true nature of the Ritual of Ascension.

This is an early pre-edit version of the story. The released version could be different.

Enjoy!

ONE

Walking distracted Wendy from the nightmares of Ascension. That was, if you could call the lurching she did walking. Pain lanced her blister raw feet with every step. The heavy bandages did little to help. She braced her IV pole after each step to catch her breath. With each pause, she'd remind herself, everyone was lying.

This was no hospital.

Not that she'd been to many hospitals, only a few and none were this clean, nor this empty. The nurses, who all wore white cloaks, did nothing but take care of Wendy. There were no other patients. Only Wendy's room had equipment in it. The only thing in each room was an open window showing the city.

Days had passed since the horrors of the mountain, the Tempters, the hunters…the feast. The first two days were a dreamless slumber, but when she awoke on the third - the new memories unleashed by the Stranger surfaced. Of course they weren't new at all, only suppressed. And some areas of the past were still murky. But, as threatened, the Stranger ripped away the scab that held her history back—and now those terrors gushed in her mind.

Memories like her mom's hand dangling over the edge of the bathtub. The water dripping, plink, plink, plink. A man's rasping snores from the bed. His jeans scrunched around his ankles. His boxer shorts dark with piss.

The memory played like a movie seen through her 12-year-old eyes. Tension built in Wendy but not about her mother, there was no doubt she was dead, but for herself. What would happen to the child left behind? Did her mom even care in the end?

On the fourth day in this 'hospital', she climbed out of her bed to do something other than remember the horrors from her past. Nurses would find her slouching in the halls when she grew too tired to go on. They'd encourage her to take it easy, congratulate her on making it further, then take her back to rest. And the memories would come back. And Wendy would walk again.

When the memories grew too unbearable, she squeezed Cassie's necklace, the marble spiral pendant. It chased away the worst memories – and reminded Wendy of the work to be done.

Find Cassie. Get forgiveness. Start again.

Her room didn't have a TV or radio. There was nothing to do but rest, remember, question, and wonder.

Everyone here was nice. Too nice. And that put her on edge more than anything.

Few spoke beyond polite smiles and curt nods. Anyone she didn't need to engage with she avoided. This wasn't the first time she'd been in a new place, and she knew the unspoken rules of all new places was to observe, don't talk, don't give anyone anything they can use against you until you know what they want.

Wendy hadn't figured out what these people wanted, yet.

The hospital gown was a funny paradox being too short for her tall body, but too wide for her emaciated frame. All the nurses remarked how easy it was to find her veins because they stuck so far out of her paper-thin skin. When they found lice, and who knows what else, nested in her hair—they shaved her bald.

Wendy didn't mind.

It was time for a new start. Horn, the man who saved her from the Sleep House, who watched over her during Ascension, said the old Wendy stayed on the mountain—might as well become the new Wendy. The old Wendy was crusty, dying under the stairs in her filth. The new Wendy—she was clean. And bathed every day to keep it that way.

But no amount of scrubbing would take away the dirt on her soul. A fact Wendy reminded herself of every moment, of every day. And as those thoughts came to her, she'd step harder to grind the pain from her feet through her body, pressing until she'd yelp to remind herself – after all she'd done - she'd never be clean.

TWO

After a week, she could make it to the chapel. No matter the time of day, people were always praying in this little room. Their monotone chanting drew her to the doorway but she'd go no further.

She'd stand outside, feeling the chants vibrate in her bones, and stare at the sapphire window glowing at the back of the small room. The window showed two men talking on a mountain of fire. One man, wreathed in black smoke, offered all there was below. The other man, dressed in a green cloak, smiled and denied the offering.

This window was the only light in the room save some flickering candles. Everyone faced the window, away from the door, kneeling, swaying, chanting. It was calming. Everyone knelt and worshiped an image she knew all too well, having faced her own version of this temptation on her own mountain. But she was offered her death instead of everything.

Horn prayed here.

He wore the brown cloak many younger people wore—but he wasn't very young. Based on the others she saw, his age suggested he should be wearing a black cloak.

The faithful's melodic chanting was a one-way conversation with God who'd listen to these people because they were here every day. Her mom always yelled at her for praying, saying it was a waste of time. Good things only happened when you made them happen, not because you asked God for them. But mom was dead—and after Ascension, Wendy didn't give a fuck what her mom thought.

But still, Wendy couldn't pray.

Could God, the true God, hear her? Would he…she…it, even listen after all those years of sin? After what she did to Yacob? To Cassie? She clenched her IV pole tighter and left before anyone saw her.

This was her ritual every day for five days. Until the sixth day when Horn wasn't at prayer. The absence of his voice left the chapel hollow—not just from the sound but his conviction in the words. The others in the chapel said the words, sang the songs, but they were simply reading, not feeling.

Without Horn, the chapel's spirit was as empty as the Sleep House. His energy buoyed the faithful. Just like her memories of Yacob buoyed her.

On the walk back, she was too busy thinking about Horn's singing, punishing herself with the pain in her feet, to notice him sitting in her room.

"Doctors say you are cleared to go," Horn said.

Wendy startled.

She stabbed her IV pole at him. The bright, sanitary lights

of her room didn't dampen the fire within. Her blood raced, her eyes wide, the fight from the mountain, the need to ward off thieves in the Sleep House, still fresh in her muscle memory.

Horn held up his hands in surrender. "Sorry, I didn't mean to scare you." He smiled, failing to cover his horror at the fight within Wendy. Everyone expected her to be weak, frail, beaten. Everyone was wrong - always. "I only came here to talk."

Wendy relaxed. Intense relief washed over her as the wait was finally over. No more wondering what these people wanted. Now was the moment of The Ask.

The Ask always came. The thing someone wanted for the thing they gave you. I'll buy you a drink if you come home with me. I'll get the room tonight if you sleep with me. I'll give you love if you give me obedience without question.

No one helped for nothing.

She sat.

A pregnant silence gathered between them.

"You were in really bad shape when we found you," Horn said then added, "on the mountain. But you were in worse shape before that. I honestly didn't think you'd make it."

He waited for a response. She withheld one.

"You committed to leaving Wendy Holowitz on the mountain. Do you still intend to fulfill that commitment?"

Wendy nodded remembering the discussion. That life is over, Horn said, and he was right. Even before the cave, her heart knew Mr. Dream was no god and the Sleep House was not a haven but a fucked-up hospice that lets you, no, encourages you to rot away with no one to give a shit about you.

"So, now what will you do?"

Wendy didn't share her plan. She only ran her fingers over Cassie's marble spiral pendant.

A helicopter rumbled passed the window. It was too far in the cityscape to see where it came from or where it went.

"I've seen you at the chapel," Horn said.

Wendy remained silent.

Horn shifted, thought, then shifted again. He was prodding her defenses. But The Ask would come, the price, and when it did, she'd not be distracted by things like chapels and commitments.

Her only commitment was to herself to survive and find Cassie. She'd find her last friend and seek the forgiveness her soul desperately needed.

And then she'd be truly clean. She could start over.

Horn continued, relaxed and feigning indifference, "The doctors say the thing you need now is a good diet and exercise. If you would like to stay with us a little longer, we can give you both. Perhaps even a purpose—that is, if you don't have anything else you'd rather do?"

Wendy said, "And?" She stayed calm.

"Take your medicine." Horn held up her cup of pills. "Do some chores around the place."

"Chores?" Wendy huffed a chuckle. "What kind of chores?"

Euphemism?

Horn shrugged. "Everyone finds their place here. Start with the library? Shelving books would help you grow your strength. Build endurance as you walk the floors. Our library is, well, it's pretty big." Horn laughed.

"And if I want to leave?" Wendy snapped at him.

Horn, non-plussed motioned to the door.

"No, I mean if I stay here until I figure out what's next. Do I have to work off my debts or something?"

Horn shook his head. "I think you'll find there are places in the world that steer you towards growth, and places that drive you to decay. I believe we are the former. We're not a prison. We're not a cult. You can leave at any time."

That's exactly what Mr. Dream said. He never meant it. He meant you can leave, but you won't survive. Yet, Horn could have killed her on the mountain. Simply doing nothing, he could have left her in the cave. So why go to all that trouble just to have her here now?

Something was off.

The helicopter flew by again. She looked, just missing it, just like before. What was it about this place?

It was familiar.

Distracted, Wendy agreed, "I'll help in the library. Do I get clothes or do all librarians here wear hospital gowns?"

Horn chuckled then called the nurse.

Nurse Leanne, Wendy's regular nurse, placed a gray cloak on the bed with neatly pressed gray pants and a matching blouse. She then removed Wendy's IV connections and bandaged the wound. "Come back if you need anything. We'll be checking in with you over the next few days," the nurse said with a smile on her lips and a glare in her eyes.

"When you are ready, get dressed and I'll meet you outside," Horn said and followed Nurse Leanne out.

Wendy stood by the window, seeing now the city was nothing more than layers of a movie set. A fake city for a fake hospital. She wasn't surprised by this, it confirmed what she assumed. Nothing here was real. Not a real city. Not a real hospital. And above all, the safety being offered was not real.

She couldn't find where the sunlight was coming from, but it filled the room with light and warmth. Even the window was hot to the touch as if baking in the summer sun all day. A fake window, with very real comfort.

Wendy went to the clothes and ran her fingers through the fine fabrics. She'd never had clothes this nice. She'd never had anyone take care of her like this, no one since Yacob. Horn saved her on the mountain. He fed her. Gave her his boots. Was he really just trying to help?

Wendy got dressed.

Horn waited at the nurse's station. Wendy clutched Cassie's necklace through the blouse, the marble spiral was cool against her skin. She was dressed, clean, and cloaked—no longer the Wendy who rotted in rags under the stairs. Death wasn't watching her here—or at least, not a Death she recognized.

Horn smiled as he saw her then motioned to the door. "Shall we?"

I hope you enjoyed these sample chapters!

Explore the Temple in THE ORDER, Faith & Deed Book 2. Discover the strange world Wendy has awoken to and the secrets it holds for her past and future.

REVIEW PLEASE

I'd really appreciate if you'd drop a review wherever you found this story. Reviews help other readers know if this story is for them. Tell people what you think they'll like about it, or what they won't like.

Thanks for helping others find my stories!

WANT MORE STORIES?

Sign up for my newsletter to read *Early Birds Pay Double*, the first appearance of Sister Wendy (who you now know as Wendy Holowitz). See what happens when she encounters a retired, stressed, unappreciated housewife who let's the monster within her finally break free.

Early Birds Pay Double is the perfect entry in the world of the Lazarus Spiral. Meet critical characters like Mr. Dream, Viola, Neil, and explore the dark secrets the Spiral unleashes in us all.

Signup to get this story along with updates and other goodies from me at https://timkulp.com/bonus/ascension

OTHER BOOKS BY T. KULP

Lazarus Spiral Series

Life Changing Yard Sale

Passages

Origins

Excess Baggage

Faith & Deed Series

Ascension

The Order

Den of Lies

Stand Alones

Good Teens Die Bad

The Hunger

BLOTS

Library of Lessons & Lies

[dis]connection

Shadows, Stains, & Secrets